THE LADY OF THE LAMPS

Vows in Vauxhall Gardens, Book 1

Daphne Quinn

© Copyright 2025 by Daphne Quinn
Text by Daphne Quinn
Cover by Kim Killion Designs

Dragonblade Publishing, Inc. is an imprint of Kathryn Le Veque Novels, Inc.
P.O. Box 23
Moreno Valley, CA 92556
ceo@dragonbladepublishing.com

Produced in the United States of America

First Edition August 2025
Trade Paperback Edition

Reproduction of any kind except where it pertains to short quotes in relation to advertising or promotion is strictly prohibited.

All Rights Reserved.

The characters and events portrayed in this book are fictitious. Any similarity to real persons, living or dead, is purely coincidental and not intended by the author.

ARE YOU SIGNED UP FOR DRAGONBLADE'S BLOG?

You'll get the latest news and information on exclusive giveaways, exclusive excerpts, coming releases, sales, free books, cover reveals and more.

Check out our complete list of authors, too!

No spam, no junk. That's a promise!

Sign Up Here

www.dragonbladepublishing.com

Dearest Reader;

Thank you for your support of a small press. At Dragonblade Publishing, we strive to bring you the highest quality Historical Romance from some of the best authors in the business. Without your support, there is no 'us', so we sincerely hope you adore these stories and find some new favorite authors along the way.

Happy Reading!

CEO, Dragonblade Publishing

PROLOGUE

LIFE HAD NEVER seemed so full of possibilities for Lady Beatrix Chichester as it did the very first time she saw the lamps illuminated at Vauxhall Pleasure Gardens.

It had taken a lot of begging and pleading to get her father to take her with him. He argued she was not out in society yet, but she reminded him that no one cared who you were at Vauxhall. He told her it was an unsuitable place for a proper young lady to go—but how could he claim that, when the Duchess of Tewksbury herself had been seen there only the previous week, with all three of her daughters?

She had seen the glass lamps in the daytime, hanging from every tree and structure, but she had not imagined the beauty of the spectacle when those lamps were lit.

As each lamp sparked into life, one after the other, as if by magic, her heart felt full, and anything seemed possible.

"Is it everything you hoped?" Papa asked as the orchestra began to play.

Beatrix looked up at him and beamed. "It's so much better, Papa. Oh, thank you so much for bringing me!" she exclaimed, sliding her arm through his and squeezing his forearm in glee.

He smiled back at her and then looked away. He never seemed entirely comfortable with her enthusiasm, although since Mama had died he had gone out of his way to make Beatrix smile.

"Let us have a drink," Papa said, nodding his head towards

the pavilion in the corner of the grove. "And then listen to some music. We can stay until supper, but no later than that…"

"Yes, Papa," Beatrix said, aware that the best way to assure Papa was likely to bring her back to the gardens again was to not cause a fuss about the time he wished to leave.

Beatrix could not wait until she was out in society properly. It was mere months until she would be presented at court—something which was necessary, as the daughter of an earl, but which terrified her—and then she would be able to attend balls and musicales and visit the theater and do all of the things that Papa generally said no to.

Because then, she would *want* to be seen everywhere. That was the point, after all. To be seen, and to find a husband.

Some evenings, when Papa had gone to White's and her governess was long in bed, Beatrix would sit by the fire and let her mind wander to the sort of man she might marry. He would be young, and handsome, and titled, of course. She imagined he would have dark hair and a smile that made her heart race.

Would she meet him at a ball? A house party in the country, like the one at which she knew her father had met her mother? Or maybe right here in London, at an event at Vauxhall Gardens?

She shivered in anticipation. Oh, how marvelous life truly was.

"Are you cold, Bea?" her father asked, frowning.

"No, Papa," she said. She certainly was not going to share her daydreams aloud. "I am simply in awe…"

She had to remind herself not to stare for too long as she stood at the entrance to the Grand Walk, the tall trees stretching into the distance. The lamps made every surface shine, and the blond hair of any young lady or gentleman seemed to shimmer. As she watched young couples taking to the dance floor, she allowed her fingertips to brush her own blond locks for a moment, taking care not to knock any of the pins out. Did her hair also glimmer in the magical light from the lamps?

Beatrix had read about the patrons of Vauxhall in the gossip columns, and she knew that as long as one could pay the shilling entrance fee, there were no other requirements that needed to be satisfied. The clothes of her fellow revelers gave some indication as to whether they were lords and ladies, merchants or maids, but it was rather thrilling to not be quite sure who one's dining companions were.

Or rather inappropriate, in Papa's mind—but as everyone important was seen at Vauxhall at some point over the summer months, he could hardly avoid it entirely.

"Is that the Earl of Haxbury I spy?" The piercing female voice carried over the sound of the orchestra, and both Beatrix and her father, Lord Haxbury, turned to see who was addressing them.

"The Duchess," Papa muttered to her, well aware that she recognized very few of the well-known faces in society, since she was not technically out yet.

"Your Grace," Papa said in his normal tone, bowing his head. "What a pleasure to see you here."

Beatrix curtsyed, feeling nervous at this social test before her.

The old lady had wiry gray curls and held up a monocle to see her conversation partners more clearly.

"May I present my daughter, Lady Beatrix Chichester, Your Grace. Beatrix, this is the Duchess of Tewksbury."

Beatrix felt her eyes widen. "An honor to meet you, Your Grace," she said, curtsying again without meaning to. "I've read…" She was about to say she had read all about her in the gossip columns, before realizing that was probably not the done thing.

Her father glared at her and the duchess appeared to be waiting for her to come out with the end of the sentence. "I have read…much about Vauxhall," she ended lamely.

The duchess nodded her head whilst narrowing her eyes. "Anything can happen in Vauxhall Gardens, or so they say!" she said with a cackle that reminded Beatrix very much of the tales of witches her mother used to tell her at bedtime. "It is your first visit, Lady Beatrix?"

"Indeed, Your Grace."

"And how do you find the gardens?"

Beatrix could not stop the smile from growing on her face. "They are wonderful, Your Grace. It feels like there is magic in the air…"

"I am afraid that magic rather fades when you grow up," the duchess said, and Beatrix did not know how to respond. Was the duchess mocking her youthful attitude? Ought she take back her comment?

She glanced up at her father, but he seemed distracted by a flame thrower on the other side of the grove, and so Beatrix was forced to make the decision herself.

"That does seem a shame," she said, hoping that she was not making a terrible social faux pas, before she had even been properly introduced to society.

"But you are right. The gardens are wonderful. My own daughters beg me to bring them here…" The woman glanced around, as though looking for her children, but instead her eyes alighted on three young men who were making their way through the crowds towards them, laughing loud enough that they could be heard above the din.

Beatrix knew it was rude to stare, but she could not help herself. All three men were handsome and full of joy, but the light from the lamps seemed to illuminate the tall, dark-haired gentleman in the center. His full lips were turned up in a smile that Beatrix found herself wanting him to direct at her. The gold buttons on his velvet waistcoat caught the light, and she noticed that he wasn't wearing a jacket, and that his shirt clung tightly to well-defined muscles in his arms.

These were not things she ought to be noticing—and definitely not things that should be taking her attention away from one of the greatest peers in the land.

"Lord Clement," the duchess said, her voice once more ringing out across the space. "And Lord Fount and Lord Linton, unless I am much mistaken."

⇒⇒⇒⟫⟪⇐⇐⇐

SPENCER STOPPED IN his tracks at the sound of his name. He had not exactly told his father where he intended to go, and so being spotted immediately was not ideal.

But then it was so fashionable to be seen at Vauxhall Gardens, he was hardly surprised that someone, especially the Duchess of Tewksbury, knew him.

"Your Grace," he said, removing his top hat and bowing deeply when he realized who had called his name. "What an honor." His companions, James and Timothy, also bowed, although as usual they let him take the lead in the conversation.

"I did not know your family were in the city," the duchess said.

"We only returned recently," Spencer said. "My brother is to wed a lady who lives close to our seat in Berkshire, and so we stayed there later than we usually would."

"Oh yes, I had read that Jack was to wed. I do love a wedding. Will it be in the city?"

"I am afraid not," Spencer said with a tight smile. He was very pleased that his brother was happy, but the constant talk of weddings was rather dull. And he did not quite trust the lady he was to marry. He did not believe she loved his brother in the way she claimed to.

"Such a shame." She glanced to her side, seeming to remember she had companions, and Spencer turned to face them. His eye was immediately caught by the shimmering of the light from the lamps upon the golden hair of the young lady who smiled at him, and blushed. He felt his mouth go dry and his skin grow warm.

"Allow me to introduce you to Lord Haxbury and his daughter, Lady Beatrix," the Duchess said, gesturing to the young lady and her father. "And these gentlemen are Lord Clement, Lord Fount and Lord Linton—all sons of friends of mine."

There was much bowing and curtsying and exchanges of greetings. Spencer was sure James and Timothy were itching to fetch a drink, and to procure a good spot before the fireworks began, but he could not walk away without asking the beautiful Lady Beatrix to dance. The exquisite lamps in the gardens eclipsed the gowns and hairstyles of nearly everyone present, but somehow they just seemed to enhance this young lady. She was practically aglow.

And he wanted a moment to bathe in that light.

"May I have the next dance, Lady Beatrix?" he asked, his tongue tripping over the words.

She blushed a deep shade of pink and looked up at her father, who frowned but then nodded his assent.

He didn't generally go to balls or choose to dance at gatherings. Such places were a hunting ground for matchmaking mamas, and at only twenty years old, Spencer had no intention of finding a wife. One day he was sure it would happen, as it had for his older brother—but then, his older brother Jack was going to be the next Marquess of Leighton, and so marrying and producing an heir was far more urgent for him than it was for Spencer, a second son.

But that night, in the fragrant gardens, with the orchestra playing in the background and entertainers at every tree-lined corner, he wanted to dance.

James and Timothy made their excuses and left as the set came to an end, and Spencer offered his arm to the lady to escort her to the dance floor for the start of the next song.

"Do you come to the gardens often, Lady Beatrix?" he asked as they began to move to the music. Despite his lack of regular practice, he had been taught all the common dances until he knew them in his sleep, and Lady Beatrix had clearly been similarly instructed too. They glided together under the lamps without needing to waste much energy on focusing on the steps.

She shook her head. "This is the first time I have visited," she said, her voice as melodic as he had imagined it might be.

"And what do you think?" he asked.

"Oh, I think it is the most magical place I have ever seen," she said, joy overtaking her face. Spencer could not help but smile back. Their hands met and he wanted to hold on, even though the dance did not require it.

On the other side of the gardens, a bell tolled, and he had to ask her, "Have you seen the Cascade yet?"

She shook her head.

"Allow me to escort you, after the dance," he said. "The way it moves, you would believe it's enchanted."

"Do you come here often then?" she asked.

"My father doesn't really approve," Spencer admitted. "But I like to come with my friends, when I can."

"I don't think mine approves either," Lady Beatrix said with a giggle. "But I have heard the prince has attended, so it cannot be so terrible!"

Spencer almost told her that Prinny being there was probably one of the reasons her father would not want his innocent daughter at the gardens, but he thought better of it. It was not a suitable comment to make to a young lady, and he would not want to be caught speaking poorly of the Prince Regent, either.

"Well I am glad he approved of you coming tonight," Spencer said eventually, and was rewarded with another blush from the young Lady Beatrix.

"I have not been presented yet," she said. "But once I am, I cannot wait to attend balls and musicales and come back to the gardens…"

"May I call on you?" Spencer asked, the words rather taking him by surprise. There was something about this beautiful, blond lady with her easy smiles and deep blushes that made him want to know her more. "Once you have been presented, I mean."

Another blush, and then she nodded. "I would like that, Lord Clement," she said.

BEATRIX NEVER WANTED the moment to end. When the dance finished, Lord Clement escorted her back to her father—but, as he had promised while they danced, he asked if he might show her the Cascade.

Papa frowned, and glanced in the direction the young lord was pointing, as if assessing how far it was, and whether he was willing to let his daughter wander so far.

"I should love to see it, Papa," Beatrix said, knowing that in spite of his concerns for her safety and reputation, he did always want to see her happy.

"For five minutes, then. But no longer—and stay where it is light. You understand me?"

"Yes, my lord," Lord Clement said, with a polite bow of his head.

He offered her his arm, and as she threaded hers through it, she thought her heart might explode. Even though his shirt sleeves and her gloves prevented their bare skin from meeting, she could feel how warm he was, how strong he was.

At seventeen years old, she had never felt this way before. She had not known that the touch of a man's hand to her own could make her whole body feel as though it were alight, nor that her mind could feel so discombobulated by the smile of a handsome gentleman.

He was everything she could have ever dreamed of—and he wanted to call on her.

Perhaps it was foolish, but she felt as though, that evening at Vauxhall Gardens, her life had truly begun.

As they approached the feat of engineering known as the Cascade—an incredible man-made waterfall, which she had heard described but never seen—she gasped.

A crowd had formed around it, but that did not impede her view. Water gushed down the huge structure, roaring impressively. The scene behind it would have been eye-catching—a beautiful vista, with a water wheel and miller's house so expertly painted they might have really been there—if it weren't for the waterfall, which eclipsed it all.

It really did seem like magic.

"I told you it was worth seeing," Lord Clement said, keeping a tight hold on her arm as the crowd around them grew.

"Most definitely!"

"They only show it for a brief period each night—that's what the bell was for," he told her knowledgeably. "And they keep it covered it the day, to make it all the more special when they do reveal it."

"It's hard to believe man could have made something so beautiful," Beatrix said, her eyes transfixed upon the scene. "I could stay here forever."

"As could I," Lord Clement said—and when she tore her eyes from the magical scene, she blushed to find he was looking at her. The look in his eyes made her feel like her whole body might melt into a puddle at his feet, and suddenly she understood why a young couple might disappear down the dark walk, which was only a few feet away… Why they would wish to be alone, with no prying eyes to judge them.

"I should take you back to your father," Lord Clement said, sorrow in his voice. "I did promise…"

Beatrix licked her lips, which had suddenly gone very dry, and nodded. "Yes, of course." He was right—and she had nearly lost her head over a handsome man. A man who quite probably did not feel the same burning through his body as she did through hers.

Papa was waiting with an anxious look on his face, which instantly relaxed at the sight of his daughter, returned safe and sound.

Lord Clement bowed once more, and reached for Beatrix's hand, pressing a kiss to the back of it. She shivered in spite of her gloves blocking any direct contact.

"I will call on you, my lady," he said softly, low enough that she did not think her father could hear, flashing that heart-stopping smile once more. "Once you are presented. I promise."

⟫⟩⟩⟩⟨⟨⟨⟪

"WHAT DO YOU mean, you've enlisted?" Spencer asked, blinking rapidly. His older brother Jack stood in the center of the room, his eyes fixed on a spot on the wall behind Spencer's head.

"Exactly what I said. I've bought a commission, and I will be leaving for France next week."

"But why?" The words coming from his brother's mouth didn't make sense. They'd been discussing the Season, and Spencer had raised the topic of which balls they should probably attend—something which didn't usually interest Spencer all that much. He had thought that by now, almost two months after that night in Vauxhall Gardens, the shining imagine of Lady Beatrix in his head would have faded, but if anything, it was brighter.

He knew she would be presented this Season.

And he wanted to be at that ball.

Then his brother had opened his mouth and announced he had enlisted, and all other conversation had fled the room.

"I feel it is my duty."

Spencer frowned. His brother had never seemed to have much of a patriotic disposition before. "But you're the son of a marquess. Hell, you'll *be* the marquess one day. I cannot see why you would feel it right to go and fight from some awful, water-logged trenches in France…"

"I have heard every argument against this from Father, Spencer. You cannot change my mind, I'm afraid. I am going."

"No," Spencer said, shaking his head. "You cannot go. You are to be wed at the end of the Season! What will your bride think?"

"Her opinion does not change things."

Spencer had never heard his brother speak so coldly. Nor had he ever felt as though something was being kept from him. The two brothers had always been close, and up until this point, Spencer had always believed his brother saw it as his duty to marry well and produce heirs to the marquisate.

This went against everything he knew of his older brother. He had never been a fighter. Never threatened a duel, never taken a fancy to pugilism, never entered into a physical fight.

He was an academic man. The perfect future marquess. Intelligent, thoughtful, and with a strong sense of duty to the name and the title.

He wasn't a soldier.

Except, apparently, he soon would be.

"Has something happened, Jack?" he asked, walking over to the drinks table to pour himself and Jack a glass of whisky.

"I made a decision, and I'm informing you of it. There is nothing else to it," Jack said, and he stormed from the room without even acknowledging the glass of amber liquid waiting for him.

Spencer took a deep breath, then sat and sipped his drink, pondering what to do.

His brother had never spoken so harshly, or so bluntly, to him before. And he had never made a rash decision in his life. Something had surely happened to make him want to leave, and Spencer needed to know what it was. And yet, if he chased after him now, he didn't think he would get any more information.

But time was ticking. If he was truly leaving in a week, then Spencer could not wait for him to return to his normal state of mind.

The image of his brother on the battlefield, alone and in danger and without any experience of fighting, sent shivers down Spencer's spine.

They had grown up together, gone to school together, attended university together. With less than two years between them, they had always been more like friends than siblings.

He couldn't let him go alone.

Unlike his brother, Spencer was known for making rash decisions, and so he let this one percolate for a while in his mind, while he drank his whisky and then spent some time pacing the library. Had they been at their country seat, he would have wandered the gardens, but he did not feel like going out into the London streets, where he would surely see someone he knew, and be forced to talk.

No, he needed to think. And he needed to think quickly.

CHAPTER ONE

Seven years later

A SMILE FLITTED across Lady Beatrix's face as Vauxhall Gardens came into view. She had not visited them in such a long time. In her first Season, she had been filled with so much disappointment at the disappearance of Lord Clement that she hadn't been able to bring herself to go.

And in her second Season, when she had discovered, through someone happening to mention it, that he had gone to fight in France, she had found her excitement over the beautiful gardens could not be renewed. The image of that handsome, kind man who had made her heart race being in the middle of a battlefield was one that haunted her at night. She knew it was silly. She didn't know him. He'd been gone a year before she'd even known that he had gone to France. She shouldn't be worrying about him.

But he came to her thoughts far more often than he ought to have done.

In her third Season, when her aunt had warned her she was in danger of becoming a spinster, destined to live alone forever, she had surprised everyone by being courted by the most notorious rake of the ton. He was dashing and shocking and Beatrix was sure he made every woman weak at the knees—even if they did not think he was a suitable prospect.

But Ambrose Trentham had singled her out, and danced with her more times than was appropriate, and set tongues wagging. In spite of his reputation, he did not complain when she hesitated to kiss him, nor when she would not allow his hands to wander where he liked.

It was exciting to be swept away in a haze of desire and gossip, to know that he wanted her, to no longer feel like a wallflower watching on while everyone else got to live their lives.

She had dreamed of excitement and romance, before she had entered society.

She had dreamed of Lord Clement.

But somewhere, it had all gone wrong.

It was approaching dusk as the boat pulled up to the pontoon, and Beatrix was offered an arm to help her from her boat, followed by her father.

He was far more fragile than he had been the last time they had visited the gardens together, seven years earlier, and Beatrix hated to notice the changes in him. The thinning, gray hair. The shaking hands. The cough that never quite went away, even in the summer months.

The last few years had not been easy on either of them. Beatrix's life had not gone the way she, or her father, expected—and although that meant more time at home with him, there was a fair amount of stress involved.

At a house party at her father's country seat, at the end of her third Season, Ambrose Trentham had proposed loudly and publicly to Beatrix, and Beatrix had agreed to be his wife.

He wasn't the man she had dreamed of, but he was young and handsome, and he wanted her.

She could be happy with him, she had been sure. Yes, his rakish ways caused gossip, but she had hoped he would become a reformed rake once they were wed.

Besides, she had not wished to go into a fourth Season still unwed. Yet here they were.

"Careful, Papa, it's a little slippery here," she said, supporting her father with her arm through his as they made their way slowly to where the beautiful lamps would be lit once dark had fallen.

When her father had suggested this excursion, she had hoped she might feel some of the magic again that she had the last time she was here, but she wondered if that was just a product of her youth.

She was no longer young, and life did not seem so exciting or full of promise.

Her fourth Season had started off well. She had been engaged, and she did not need to worry about trying to attract a husband, as she had done every year prior. Even Aunt Elspeth had been pleased about that—although she did not keep her negative comments about Beatrix's intended to herself.

But by the middle of that Season, Beatrix found herself purchasing black mourning clothes, her life turned upside down.

"I always said he was no good," Aunt Elspeth had said, showing her customary lack of tact. "Who gets themselves killed in a duel these days, honestly? It's illegal for one. And downright foolish for another."

Beatrix had kept her mouth shut and sipped her lemonade and tried to hold back tears.

Had she loved Ambrose?

She wasn't truly sure. He had stirred up passion with her, that was for sure. And he had been fun and carefree and so full of life. And he had wanted her. She had envisioned her life with him. They were going to be married.

And in a stupid, drunken, foolhardy instant, he was gone.

And she was alone.

Not a widow, because she had never been a wife. Just another lady looking for a husband. Again. *Still.*

So here she was. Entering her seventh season, unwed, tainted by her association with a rake—however chaste their courtship had been—and his subsequent death, followed by her own mourning period.

"I think I need to sit down, dear," Papa said, and Beatrix found them seats, before excusing herself to get them refreshments. She worried about Papa. His health had declined so rapidly, and the doctors didn't seem to know why. They threw around scary words and tried increasingly aggressive and expensive treatments, but no one ever seemed to have a solution that would actually cure him of whatever it was that ailed him. Worse, it was possible that all that ailed Papa was that he was growing old, and there was no cure for that.

She stood by the refreshment table and took in the scene around her. So many important people filled the gardens, which were still as popular as they had been when they opened. Young men and women, eager to find their match. Matchmaking mamas and long-suffering fathers and maiden aunts…

Could one be a maiden aunt, if one had no siblings and therefore no nieces and nephews?

Beatrix sighed. This was not what she had imagined. When she had stepped into the shining light of society, she had thought her life would be marvelous. But the only other men to offer her marriage had been old enough to be her father. Her grandfather, even, in some cases.

Life certainly didn't hold such magic anymore.

CHAPTER TWO

A S THE BOAT approached the gardens, Spencer tried to summon up some enthusiasm. His friends had insisted that Vauxhall Gardens was still the place to be, even though their popularity had surely been waning.

Putting on a top hat and heading to drink and dance was so far removed from the life he had lived for the last few years that Spencer found it hard to acclimatize. He'd seen men run through with swords and disemboweled in front of him, watched starvation and illness ravage a camp of soldiers.

He'd come back physically whole, but mentally he did not see how he could ever be the carefree man he had been when he'd left to fight in France. Since returning, he had secluded himself at home, not wanting to see anyone or to hear his new title.

But eventually, his friends had persuaded them to join him.

"Come on, Leighton. A couple of drinks will put you in the mood for frivolity."

Spencer wasn't sure he would ever be in the mood for frivolity again. He still couldn't bear to hear anyone address him as "Lord Leighton", and yet, of course, they did.

Because that *was* his title.

He was the Marquess of Leighton, and he would be until the day he died and his heir—whomever that might be, should there even be one—took on the title.

He followed his friends into the gardens, trying to remember the excitement he had felt when he had visited them in his youth. There had been one magical night, when he had been there with the very same friends, James and Timothy, where he'd met a woman who remained in his thoughts for a long time. Even in France, during the grimmest, darkest moments, the way the lights had glinted off her beautiful golden hair had shone in his memories like a beacon of what was once good in his life. Not that he'd expected to experience that goodness ever again.

But there was no point in thinking back to that night. That was in the time before. When he was confident of the path that lay before him. When his father was the Marquess, his brother primed to take his place when he unfortunately passed.

"Come on Spencer, they'll be lighting the lamps soon," Timothy called from up ahead. Spencer had no excuse for lagging behind, other than a lack of enthusiasm. He'd not sustained any serious wounds while at the front, somehow.

And yet, Jack…

He forced back the tide of emotion that always threatened to overwhelm him when he thought of Jack. His older brother. The sensible, thoughtful one of the two of them. The heir to the marquisate.

They'd thought the battle was over. The guns had fallen silent, and the wounded were groaning where they lay, hoping for help or for the mercy of death. Jack hadn't been able to leave a friend dying mere feet away from their trench. He'd become far more impulsive during their time in France. Spencer had followed him onto the battlefield, of course; Jack was the whole reason he was in France, after all.

And then, as they were dragging the groaning man back to safety, the musket ball had found its way into Jack's chest.

One minute he had been alive and talking and telling his comrade that everything was going to be well. And the next the life had gone from his eyes, and his blood was covering the soldier they were dragging, and Spencer.

"See?" James said, handing him a glass of something not nearly alcoholic enough. "Aren't you glad you came?"

The honest answer was "no", but Spencer didn't feel he could say that. His friends weren't trying to make him miserable. They had made it clear that they didn't think it was healthy for him to stay locked away in his London townhouse all the time.

They had suggested he head to the country, even though the fashionable time of year for doing so had passed—but he couldn't bring himself to.

Their country seat just reminded him of his father, who had lost his battle against old age the previous year, and his brother, who should have inherited.

While the townhouse held many memories, it had at least been somewhere he had spent plenty of time in the Season without his father or brother. It was hard to get used to the servants calling him Lord Leighton, but other than that, he could pretend nothing had changed.

"Indeed," Spencer said, feeling like an answer was expected of him. The lamps were lit, and the assembled crowd *oohed* and *ahhed*. Spencer wanted to feel awed by the sight. He had—before. But now… He hated how the war had changed him. But what joy could he find in lamps when he had seen so much death and destruction?

He'd dragged his brother and the fallen soldier—Lieutenant Johnson—back to base camp, somehow avoiding any musket balls himself. His eyes had stung with unshed tears, but he had forced himself to continue, hoping in his heart that the medics might be able to magically and miraculously do something to save his beloved older brother even as his rational mind knew Jack was beyond hope.

"Did you see that young lady in the blue dress?" James said, nodding his head towards the refreshment table. "I'm going to ask her to dance."

"Your father nagging you to wed again?" Timothy asked with a chuckle.

Times had definitely changed. The last time Spencer had been there, his friends had no thoughts of marriage at all. Both had planned to put it off until a much later date—but that "much later date" was fast approaching. Indeed, it may have already passed.

Timothy was already betrothed to a young woman Spencer had not yet met, and James was clearly planning to head up the aisle soon after him. He wouldn't be asking eligible young women to dance otherwise.

"You should dance too, Spencer. Take your mind off everything for tonight. I know being a marquess is a heavy burden, but it does not mean you cannot have fun."

Spencer struggled to explain to them exactly why being the marquess weighed so heavily upon him. It wasn't the work associated with the role, for he had an estate manager who was very experienced, and he was willing to learn how to manage the paperwork. And it wasn't that it curtailed the enjoyable activities in his life—because his days of drinking and gambling and raking through London were long behind him.

No, it was a burden because it didn't feel like it should be his. The title, the money, the estates, the duty to pass on the title to an heir one day… none of that had been meant to fall to him.

And perhaps, if he'd done a better job of protecting Jack in France, it wouldn't have.

"Just leave me to my misery," Spencer snapped at Timothy, and then immediately felt guilty. None of it was Timothy's fault. "My apologies. Please, go and dance. I will join you after this drink…"

They hurried away, and Spencer couldn't blame them. Who would want to be someone so angry and miserable, a shell of his former self?

He hated that war for so many things. For taking Jack. For filling his head with images of dying men. For haunting his nightmares. For irrevocably changing who he was.

Spencer watched his friends dancing with beautiful young women under the light of the glass lamps as he knocked back another drink. If he left and went home now, it would only be to sit in his library with a bottle of whisky, hoping that he could stop the nightmares from coming if he was drunk enough.

He closed his eyes for a moment and tried to picture that night, seven years earlier, when he had danced with the enchanting Lady Beatrix. Her name was imprinted on his mind even all these years later, even with all the horrors he had witnessed. When she smiled, it had made his heart feel like it might burst. One perfect evening with his lady of the lamps—and then he had never seen her again.

She was surely married by now. Such a beautiful, sweet woman would not have remained on the marriage mart for long after her debut. He had considered asking around after her, but had concluded there was no point. He didn't know her, and she probably didn't even remember him.

She was most probably at home right now with some adoring husband and a couple of children in the nursery in a life so far from his own it was hard to even imagine it.

When he opened his eyes, he thought he was seeing things.

He did not know how, but somehow his imagination had conjured the vision of Lady Beatrix before him.

Just like that night seven years earlier, she seemed to glow under the lanterns. Her blond hair still shone, and when she smiled at the man whose arm was entwined with hers, it made Spencer's heart feel warm.

It was the strongest positive emotion he had felt in years.

His eyes slid to her companion, and he was surprised and pleased to note that the gentleman was her father, Lord Haxbury, and not a husband. That didn't mean one did not exist, of course...but it made it far easier for him to ask her to dance without incurring anyone's wrath.

Which he decided he had to do.

No, it wouldn't change anything. He was a broken, bitter and twisted man, and he'd danced with her once seven years ago and never seen her again.

But if he could relive a little of the magic and romance of that night… well, perhaps he could start to look to the future. He hurried over before he could change his mind and stopped abruptly before them to remove his top hat and bow.

When he rose, Lady Beatrix was staring at him, her eyes wide and her mouth forming an "o".

"Lord Haxbury," Spencer said, his heart jumping at the notion that she recognized him. "We met several years ago. It's a pleasure to see you again."

Lord Haxbury's eyes were cloudy with age, and although he smiled, there was no recognition there. "Indeed. A pleasure to see you, Lord—"

"Clement," Lady Beatrix whispered, her eyes focused on Spencer.

She remembers me. He hadn't expected to feel so intoxicated by the fact that she clearly remembered their encounter as vividly as he did. The weight on his heart lifted and for brief moment—half a breath, at least, he was the young man he'd been and not the bitter husk of a human that he'd become. He was whole.

CHAPTER THREE

S URELY THIS HAD to be a dream.

Beatrix had imagined seeing him a thousand times before. Often her imaginings had been in this place, where they had danced under the light of a thousand lamps… But she had never actually expected to see him here again.

Not now, seven years after that magical night.

He bowed his head, and his smile was just as heart-stopping now as it had been then.

"I am Lord Leighton, now, but I'm honored you remember me, Lady Beatrix." Beatrix could not stop the blush that spread across his cheeks as he said her name.

He remembers me.

The hurt when he did not call had faded over the years—especially when she had realized he had gone to France to fight.

The relief at knowing he had not perished on the battlefield, as so many young men had, that he was here, alive and well and smiling at her…

"May I have the next dance?"

She already felt shocked that he was here, in the flesh, not in her imagination. But surely she was dreaming that he was asking her to dance?

Father looked up at her with that faraway smile he often got now. He was no longer so concerned about whom she danced with; perhaps he had given up hope of her ever getting married. It had certainly been a while since anyone had asked to escort her onto the dance floor. At almost five-and-twenty, she did not think anyone expected her to suddenly make a fine match. Not anymore.

"Go and have fun, Bea. I'll take a seat over there." Papa's arm slipped from hers, and she watched him walk away, suddenly feeling rather shy.

She didn't know Lord Clement—or Lord Leighton, as he now was. She tried to remember what they had discussed. Had she known he was in line for a different title? She had pored over every detail of their conversation in her mind over the years and she did not think that piece of information was part of it.

The musicians began to play the next song, and Lord Leighton offered his hand. Butterflies filled Beatrix's stomach as she accepted, feeling the years and her weariness of society shedding as she took to the dance floor.

"I heard you were in France," she said, when there was a moment for conversation. Because what did one say to a man one had danced with once and then thought about for years after?

Lord Leighton nodded. "Yes. When we last met... I did not know that I would end up enlisting. So I can only apologize for not following through and calling on you, like I promised."

"Of course," Beatrix said, trying to pretend that it had been of no consequence. "Have you been back long?" She wanted to ask how he was now Lord Leighton, but she did not wish to be rude, or to bring up some painful event that had presumably led to him inheriting the title.

"It has been two months, I believe," he said, faltering in the steps slightly. It was a newer dance, and she wondered if he had ever danced it before. She was certain there was not much call for dancing on the battlefield.

"I haven't seen you at any of the functions this Season..." She wished she could take the words back as soon as she had uttered them. He would think she spent every ball and musicale looking for him, like some pining wallflower.

The slight truth to that notion only made it more pathetic.

"I don't much care for society," he said shortly.

His tone cut off Beatrix's next question. He had clearly changed in the seven years since they had last met. Then he'd had a real *joie de vivre*, and she'd gotten the impression that he would attend any event as long as there was a chance of a good time.

He had asked her to dance, but he didn't really seem to want to be there.

Maybe he had changed… Or maybe she had never really known him at all. Which, of course, she had not. But she'd felt like she had…

⟫⟪

EVEN THOUGH HE found it hard to make light conversation, which had once been something he had enjoyed partaking in, the dance with Lady Beatrix was the happiest moment he'd had in years.

He'd noticed that she did not correct him when he called her Lady Beatrix, which gave him hope that somehow she was not yet wed—even though such an idea was ridiculous. And really, why did it matter? He wasn't in any fit state to marry. He wouldn't shackle anyone to such a miserable husk of a man—let alone a woman as bright and effervescent as Lady Beatrix.

But still, it made him happy, for a moment. And that was longer than he'd been happy in quite some time.

When their hands met, he felt a spark ignite something within him that he'd thought was long dead.

Hope, perhaps.

"The lamps are as beautiful as ever, are they not?" *Just as you are.* He couldn't say what he was thinking; it would be too scandalous. She was a well-bred lady, and he was a marquess.

But she was just as beautiful as she had been that night. The years had only enhanced her beauty.

Lady Beatrix sighed and glanced up at them, not missing a

step in the dance. Spencer only hoped she hadn't noticed the number of times he had misstepped. He really ought to have made sure it was a dance he was confident in before taking to the floor.

"Yes. I confess I have not visited often, but I have always remembered the magic of the lamps on that night we met."

When the dance came to an end, he escorted her back to her father, but found he was not keen to rejoin his friends. He wanted to enjoy the warmth he felt just being in Lady Beatrix's presence for a little longer.

"Do you plan to stay in London for the Season?" Lady Beatrix asked.

"I believe so. And perhaps afterwards, too. I do not wish to retire to the countryside just yet…"

She nodded as though she understood, but there was no way she could—and Spencer did not wish to mar the evening with his misery over the death of both his brother and his father, so he did not explain any further. "And you?"

"Oh yes. Although we may go to Bath to take the waters at some point." She glanced at her father, who had remained seated and certainly looked frail. He felt sorry for the man, but was glad that it wasn't Beatrix whose health required the waters.

The sight of Timothy and James approaching made his heart drop a little. He didn't want this moment to end—but he didn't seem to be able to make polite conversation anymore.

They both stopped and bowed, looking to Spencer for an introduction. They clearly did not remember meeting Lord Haxbury and his daughter. But then, why should they? They hadn't been so affected by the meeting as Spencer, although they had teased him about it back then.

"Lord Haxbury, and his daughter Lady Beatrix," Spencer said. "May I present Lord Fount and Lord Linton, old friends of mine."

"A pleasure to meet you," Lady Beatrix said with a curtsy. Spencer couldn't help but wonder if she remembered them from that night, since she clearly remembered him. A sizzle from a torch caught their attention then, and they turned to see what it was.

"Oh good, the fireworks are about to start," Lady Beatrix exclaimed, clapping her hands together and beaming.

Her joy distracted Spencer from what was about to occur; he was too busy looking at the beautiful smile on her face to think about what was about to happen next. But then, the first flash of light and crash of an explosion made Spencer's heart seize up as panic filled him. *Take cover!* screamed in his head, along with the echoes of men's shouts and the whinnies of panicked horses. *Get out of here!*

The sound of gunshots filled his mind, and fear filled his body, making his only options fight or flight.

And he had no weapon, no way to protect himself, no way to avoid joining the mound of groaning, dying bodies that would surely be present once the explosions had subsided.

He was in the world of his nightmares. So he ran.

CHAPTER FOUR

PAPA HADN'T EVEN noticed Lord Leighton running off, but Beatrix was sure everyone else had. She had no idea what she had done or said wrong. One moment, she'd felt as though she was walking on air—dancing with the man she'd thought she would never see again, and then watching the incredible firework display light up the sky.

The next, he had bolted. She had called out to him—something which probably drew even more attention to his hasty departure—but it was like he hadn't heard her.

Or hadn't wanted to.

Was it something I said? she wondered all the way home. Once in the carriage, Papa had fallen asleep, and the ensuing quiet had only given her more time to think about the embarrassing end to what had been a magical night.

For a brief moment, she'd thought that her dreams had come true. It was a foolish daydream, she could see that now. But when he had appeared as if by magic and they had danced under the glow of the lamps, it had seemed like time had been turned back.

Like she had another chance at the happiness she had always expected her life would be full of.

And then he ran away.

Perhaps he was married, and felt awkward telling her.

Perhaps he was just being polite by dancing with her. And yet he had remembered her, after all those years…

Maybe it had suddenly dawned on him that she was a spinster, not a woman he wanted to be courting.

Sadness settled over her as she went to bed that evening. Her maid Jemima commented on how quiet she was, but Beatrix did not explain why.

Jemima was her closest confidante, and yet she did not want to share how foolish she had been, imagining a man like Lord Leighton would still be interested in her after seven long years, and dreaming of some perfect future based on one dance.

She had thought she had grown out of such nonsense. And so she had—until the handsome man she had kept in her mind for so long suddenly reappeared.

And then promptly disappeared.

Rather, he had run. Without saying good night, even. He had just turned tail as if being chased by demons.

It was a rather extreme reaction to whatever she had done wrong, she thought as she lay in bed, unable to sleep.

But he surely had his reasons.

And since there was no way she was going to call on a gentleman, even if she had a clue where he was residing, she resolved to forget him.

Instead she needed to focus on building a future for herself. If she wanted a husband and children, and not to be a spinster for the rest of her days, she could not spend her life wishing for a fairytale.

⋙✕⋘

A WEEK AFTER the ill-fated trip to Vauxhall Gardens, Beatrix received a startling visit which forced any romantic notions from her mind.

"A caller to see you, Lady Beatrix," their butler Samson announced as he opened the door to the drawing room. Both Beatrix and her father sat up a little straighter; it had been a long time since young men had called upon Beatrix during the visiting hour.

Foolishly, Beatrix allowed her heart to hope, just for a moment, that it was Lord Leighton.

But the gentleman shown in was no young man, and he was very definitely not Lord Leighton.

He took off his top hat, revealing a balding head with scattered gray hairs across it, and bowed.

"Lord Haxbury, Lady Beatrix. It is a pleasure to see you again."

Beatrix had to rack her brains to try to remember seeing this man before. He had to be older than her father, and no name came springing to her mind.

"Lord Filton," Papa said, more alert than he normally was. "What brings you into town during the Season? I thought you avoided it like the plague!"

Both men guffawed, and Beatrix was left none the wiser as to who the guest was.

"I shall call for some tea and cake, my lord," she said, curtsying politely before reaching for the bell cord.

"Excellent. My, you have grown up, Lady Beatrix."

His eyes raked up and down her body and she fought the urge to shiver in discomfort.

"Beatrix," Papa said, as though suddenly remembering her existence. "You remember the Earl of Filton, do you not? We used to visit him at his country estate in Wiltshire."

"Oh yes, of course," Beatrix lied. She didn't remember the earl or his estate—but she didn't want to be rude, or force her father to go into some long trip down memory lane to explain the connection to her. This gentleman was clearly there to see her father, and so Beatrix would smile politely, drink her tea, and work on her needlework while the two men conversed.

"It's been years," Papa said as the tea was poured before him. "Why, Bea must have been a little girl when you last saw her. And my Emily still alive..." Sadness passed across his face, as it always did when Mama was mentioned, and Beatrix decided to move the conversation along before he could become morose. These days, it wasn't easy to pull him out of a maudlin mood once he had sunk into it.

"Do you not care for Town during the Season, Lord Filton?" she asked, pausing in her embroidery of a delicate flower in the corner of a handkerchief to address him. His blue eyes looked as though they had paled with age, and she found herself wondering how he and her father had become friends, since he clearly was too old to be a school chum.

"No. Too many people, too much noise…give me free reign of my estate any day!"

Beatrix smiled and nodded. While she liked the countryside, she couldn't agree with him; the hustle and bustle of town when everyone descended upon it was the most exciting part of the year.

"But something's changed?" Papa asked.

"Well. You may have heard that Lady Filton passed away last year?"

Beatrix had, of course, not heard, for she hadn't remembered of the existence of Lord Filton until that very morning—but Papa nodded sadly as though it were not news to him.

She was surprised, however, at how coolly the Earl mentioned the death of his late wife. Referring to her as "Lady Filton", even to a supposed close friend, did not endear him to Beatrix.

"I'm sorry to hear that," Beatrix murmured, wondering why her death had led to his arrival in town. She presumed it had been more than a year since her passing, since he was not wearing a mourning arm band—but then perhaps he did not feel the need to follow the custom.

"It's naturally time for me to find a new wife, and so I must endure the social Season!" Lord Filton laughed, and her father did too, and Beatrix felt sick to her stomach.

Did marriage really mean so little to men that when a wife died, the only importance was to find another one as soon as was socially acceptable? Was this the world that her future happiness depended on? She had seen how deeply her father mourned her mother, and still did—and yet he laughed along with this earl all the same.

She knew she needed to look at the world less romantically, but one hoped for a little romance in marriage, surely…

"Perhaps we will see you at the Pollark ball next week then?" Papa said. Beatrix hadn't even known he planned to attend the ball, but she supposed it was important they still went to as many functions as possible during the Season. If she wanted a husband, that was.

Although right now, she wasn't entirely sure that she did.

"I'll be there. I believe my daughter and her husband will be in attendance too."

"Oh goodness. In my head, Natasha is still a little girl!"

The earl laughed. "She is quite grown, and married too—but I actually meant Charlotte. Natasha is still in the countryside, after her confinement. Her second child, and a son this time, thank goodness!"

With every minute that passed, Beatrix disliked this man more.

"I am very much looking forward to marrying a young woman who will present me with a son," Lord Filton said, a leering smile upon his face. "After all, I don't need to be young myself to become a father again!"

Beatrix could only stand, horrified, as her father laughed along with the vile man.

CHAPTER FIVE

S PENCER SPENT A week trying to put the fireworks from his mind, and another trying to forget his embarrassing behavior.

He had thought, once he was home from France, that the nightmares would stop. That loud noises wouldn't make him jump out of his skin. That life could return to at least a semblance of normality—albeit without his father or his brother around anymore.

But no. The first evening for months where he had actually felt like himself, and those damned fireworks had sent him running for his home.

James and Timothy had turned up at his townhouse an hour after the fireworks, hammering on the door and demanding entrance to see that he was well—which only made everything worse.

Each pound of their fists on the door only brought the images of the soldiers scattered across the battlefield more sharply into his mind.

His butler had tried and failed to send them away, and it was only after a shaking Spencer asked his valet, Allan, to plead with them to leave, that they finally did. And Spencer slept fitfully for the next thirteen hours, reliving the horrors of war and the terror he had felt so frequently over the last seven years.

He hadn't wanted society to see how broken he was. Perhaps he should have kept himself locked away, and not listened to his friends telling him that he needed to spend some time around others.

And he definitely shouldn't have asked Lady Beatrix to dance. If he hadn't done that, she wouldn't have witnessed him fleeing from the loud bangs. He didn't want to look weak in front of anyone, but especially her. It made no sense, really. She was a woman he'd danced with once, long ago. She did not know him, and he did not know her, aside from a few pleasantries.

And yet the image of her, glowing beneath those lamps, that smile that made his heart feel like it was glowing too…it was hard to get it out of his mind.

He agreed to a drink at the club with Timothy and James a fortnight after the debacle, mainly to stop them from knocking on the door and his butler from having to turn them away.

There was a knot in his stomach as he walked into the dimly lit room. The candles had only recently been lit, and there wasn't really enough light coming from them or the dusky sky outside. Not for the first time, he wished he could feel as at ease around his friends as he always had done.

Every evening they had spent together back then had been full of laughter, good-natured teasing, and light hearts.

Not anymore.

Spotting them at a table in the corner of the room, he forced himself to approach.

"Good evening." He knew he was being far more formal than he would normally be, but it was hard to dispel the awkwardness he felt after the evening at Vauxhall Gardens.

"Good to see you," James said with a broad grin.

"Are you—*uh*…feeling better?" Timothy asked.

His fragile mental state was not something for discussion with anyone, let alone his boyhood friends, but he had to give them some sort of explanation for the erratic behavior they had witnessed from him.

"Yes. Thank you." He signaled for a whisky. Was his answer the truth? He wasn't sure. He was definitely better than he had been that night, but would he ever be fully healed? "The fireworks…took my mind back to France."

Dear God, he hoped that would be enough for them. He didn't want to answer any questions or explain further. The simple admission that he could not hear the explosions of fireworks without his mind spiraling into panic was hard enough. He took a large swig of his whisky the second it was brought, and prayed the conversation would move on.

"I don't believe you are the only one so afflicted…" Timothy said cautiously.

Spencer pressed his eyes closed momentarily. He knew others who were just as damaged. More so, even—and in body, as well as in mind.

"It will pass," he insisted sharply, as if he did not spend every day terrified that it never would.

"Of course," James agreed.

They sipped whisky in awkward silence for a few minutes, and Spencer wondered if this was worse than the fireworks or his reaction to them.

"I heard there's to be a high-stakes card game at the Pollark Ball tomorrow night," Timothy finally said. Relief washed over Spencer at the chance to talk about anything but his bloody weakness when it came to loud noises.

"Oh? How high stakes are we talking?" James asked.

Timothy leaned forward and lowered his voice. "Scandalously high stakes, so I heard."

Spencer frowned. "I thought the Pollark Ball was the sort that débutantes frequented?" He hadn't intended to attend, but he was sure he remembered seeing the name on an invitation in the pile of invitations that had stacked up since he had returned home from France.

"Well." James leaned back in his chair with a smug smirk upon his face. "It always was. And it will still attract that crowd. But with all the Pollark girls married off, it seems Mr. Pollark is keen to make things a bit more interesting at his yearly ball!"

"Well, you'll be in the ballroom lining up dances, won't you, since you need to think about wedding soon," Timothy teased him.

James rolled his eyes. "Have I missed the date of the wedding between you and the delightful Miss Catherine Bollington? 'Betrothed' is not the same as wed, you know Timothy."

Timothy groaned. "Don't I know it. None of the privileges, eh?"

The three men laughed, and ordered more whisky, and it almost felt like old times.

Almost.

But Spencer could never quite rid his mind of his woes. That he was not the man meant to be the Marquess of Leighton. That his brother ought to be sitting here, wed and settling down to the task of producing the heir. Or perhaps he'd even have an heir already, since it had been seven years since they left for France.

Spencer couldn't imagine ever tying a woman to a life with a man who jumped at his own shadow. It wouldn't be right. He had to be the marquess, because people were relying on him to manage the estates and provide jobs—but he had made his peace with the fact that once he was gone, the title would pass to some distant cousin.

He had a vague idea who it would be, but he hadn't bothered to look up his lineage in his father's records to be sure. After all, what would it matter? He would be dead and buried.

In his most morbid moments, he thought he ought to be already. That he should have joined Jack in dying in a trench in France—or died instead, so his brother would be in England, fulfilling the role he was born to inherit.

And yet…

As Timothy and James joked about half-dressed singers and winning favors in a game of cards, Spencer could not get the ethereal Lady Beatrix from his mind.

He could never imagine tying some woman to him for life. But when he had briefly imagined marriage, there was only one woman who danced through his thoughts. Even if he was only torturing himself by picturing how magical she had looked under those lamps…

CHAPTER SIX

S PENCER DID NOT attend the Pollark Ball. He considered it, but told himself it was too late to turn up without having responded to the invitation.

In truth, he knew that they would have happily welcomed him, as an elusive marquess—and especially considering he was unwed, and there would be plenty of young ladies at the ball looking for husbands.

But he was not looking for a wife, and he did not wish to have people point and stare and gossip about his strange behavior in the gardens. He had avoided reading any of the gossip columns, in case they conjectured about his sudden exit, and turning up to the ball just seemed like a disaster waiting to happen.

He did meet his friends for a drink again the following day though, and started promenading through St James's Park on fine mornings when spring took the chill out of the air, so that he didn't turn entirely into a hermit again.

Lady Beatrix remained on his mind. He knew he could call on her, since they had been introduced, but he couldn't bring himself to. She would expect that he was interested in courting her—as he would have been had he managed to call on her before he had left for France—and he didn't want to disappoint.

So when, on a particularly pleasant March morning, he saw her across the busy park, he found himself unsure as to what to do.

He wanted to speak to her, but he didn't seem to be very good at making conversation anymore. And if he did speak with her, how would he possibly explain his abrupt departure from Vauxhall Gardens?

But if he walked away, and did not speak with her…could he forgive himself?

He continued on his path, knowing that if she did the same, they would certainly run into each other. She was promenading with a maid, and he wondered if her father was too frail to join her on such walks now. He certainly looked like age had taken its toll on him when Spencer had seen him again.

He could tell by her eyes widening and her jaw clenching the moment that she spied him. He couldn't blame her for not wanting to speak with him. He forced his features to remain neutral, slowing down as he approached her and removing his top hat.

"Good day, Lady Beatrix," he said with a bow.

"Lord Leighton," she replied softly, curtsying and not quite meeting his eye. Was she embarrassed to be seen with him, after his behavior the other night? Was she worried that onlookers might think they were a courting couple?

"I hope you are well." It was the only comment Spencer could think to make. "And your father, too?"

"Yes, thank you. And you…are you well?"

Her piercing blue eyes finally met his and a jolt traveled down his spine. What a question. He knew she was asking whether he had recovered from his strange behavior, but for him it went so much deeper.

He wasn't well. And no matter how much he wanted to be, he didn't know if he ever would be again.

But that was not a topic for polite conversation.

"Yes, thank you. Fine weather we're having, is it not?"

THE CONVERSATION WAS stilted and awkward, and Beatrix was sure Jemima was listening in to every word with rapt interest.

After all, this was the gentleman that Beatrix had waxed lyrical about, once upon a time. And now they could only discuss the weather...

"Yes. Beautiful. I do like to walk in the park when it is dry," Beatrix said.

When she had first seen him, casually strolling along the very same path as she was, her heart had almost stopped in shock. Then it had raced faster than it ought as she had tried to think what to say, and wondered whether he would stop to speak to her after leaving her at the fireworks.

Oh, how she wanted to ask him why he had left. But she couldn't. It would not be polite to do so—and besides, what if he were honest with her in answering, and she didn't like the answer?

And so they stood awkwardly conversing as happy young couples wandered along, some newlywed and some still with chaperones trailing behind them.

Beatrix had walked through this park for years, often with her father, and she had always looked upon those couples in the first flush of courtship and wondered how it would feel when it was her. And, when Ambrose had flirted with her and courted her, she had felt a little like she had imagined those couples would feel.

Now she couldn't look at those couples without feeling rather disgruntled. But she would have settled for feeling disgruntled rather than the next emotion to accost her: *horror*.

For her father's friend the Earl of Filton was speedily approaching her—and he had made it all too apparent at the Pollark Ball that he considered her an excellent candidate to become the next Lady Filton.

An idea that made her want to be sick.

And yet... What options did she truly have? If she wanted to be a wife and mother, and have an estate to run, might she have to settle for a man who was already a grandfather?

Father didn't seem horrified by the idea... And that was almost harder to stomach than Lord Filton's lecherous smirks.

The handsome young earl before her didn't even seem to want to make conversation with her, if she read the way he kept looking off into the distance correctly.

Her options were pitifully limited.

To be that girl in Vauxhall Gardens again, with her whole life ahead of her, full of possibilities…

"Well. Good day, Lady Beatrix," Lord Leighton said with a stiff nod. As she watched him stride off into the distance, Beatrix wanted to call out and ask for an explanation. His awkwardness around her felt like such a rejection; like a punishment for something she had done wrong, and yet she had no idea what it was.

And why was she pining for a man she didn't know? It was the fantasy of him in her head; the perfect memory of a night so long ago that she surely could not keep all the details straight in her head.

She needed to let go.

"Lady Beatrix!" Lord Filton called, raising a hand in greeting. His cheeks were reddened from his increased speed, and his calling of her name ensured she could not walk off and pretend she had not seen him.

She greeted him with a sinking heart. "Good morning, Lord Filton," she murmured politely, though she felt anything *but* good.

"I thought I might walk you home, if you were headed that way. I was actually planning to call on you…"

Beatrix forced a smile on her face. There was no use in being rude. She didn't want to marry this man, to step into the role of mother to children older than she was, and become a grand-mother to babies before she'd had any of her own—but if he was her only option, she did not wish to offend him.

Apparently, if her interaction with Lord Leighton was any indication, she could do that without knowing how.

"It is a lovely morning, is it not," she said as they began the walk back home. Banal conversation could in no way be considered offensive.

"Oh, yes. Well, too warm really. In the countryside there is always some fresh air to balance these things…"

Beatrix hid her sigh and tried not to picture what her future held.

CHAPTER SEVEN

SEVERAL DAYS AFTER meeting Lord Leighton in the park, Beatrix was losing all hope. Lord Filton was becoming more insistent, and she was desperate to avoid what was probably inevitable. "I think we should go to Bath, Papa," she said as they sat in the library after supper. A fire was roaring in the grate, and Papa looked as though he might drop off to sleep at any moment. But Beatrix didn't want to wait to discuss the plan. The idea had been on her mind for a few days, and the more tenacious Lord Filton became, the more she wanted to leave town.

"Now? In the middle of the Season? It's not really..."

Beatrix took advantage of Papa trailing off to jump in with her reasons. "I know that. But it is far from my first Season. I do not think anyone is really paying attention to me. And you have been struggling with your health for some time now. Perhaps taking the waters will help you."

Papa screwed up his face and Beatrix shoved her needlework to one side. "It's worth a try, Papa. There are balls in Bath, too— it's not as though I shan't be able to socialize at all..."

"But Lord Filton..."

Beatrix bit her bottom lip. She had thought Papa favored his suit, but she had been hoping it was not true. How could he think to marry her off to such an old man? She knew they were friends, but she found Lord Filton odious. And she could not bear the thought of sharing his bed...

She had come to the conclusion that perhaps if he was the only option, it was not an option she wanted.

"Papa. He is a pleasant man"—she lied in order not to upset her father—"—but he is too old to be my husband."

Papa sank down in his chair, looking even smaller than he normally did. It was sad how age had taken a formidable man and made him diminutive. Beatrix struggled to picture him as he had been in her youth.

"I know. But Bea, sweetheart... You haven't had an offer in quite some time."

Of course, she knew that was the truth. And she had been very honest with herself that she was aging fast and no longer a débutante who young men would be clamoring to dance with.

But there was a difference in knowing it and hearing one's father confirm it. That her only hope was a man old enough to be her grandfather. Tears filled Beatrix's eyes, and she had to look away so that her father would not see.

It broke her heart.

"You know I would happily have you by my side forever. I have no wish to send you off to be wed to anyone. But my health is not what it was..."

More tears filled her eyes at this morbid statement, and she knew she could not hold them back for long.

"Papa..." There was so much she wanted to say, but the knot in her throat prevented her from doing more than speaking his name.

"It is the truth. We do not know how long I have left, and I do not wish you to be alone and unprotected in this world. With no husband, no brothers, no sons... It's a harsh world for a female alone, even one of your status."

What he said was sensible, and Beatrix knew that, even though she did not wish to admit it. If one was a wealthy widow, that was one thing, but being alone in the world and having never been married was an entirely different matter...

"I cannot pass my title to you. And you know I would if I

could. But when I do go—no, sweetheart, do not get upset, it will happen sometime—then the new heir, my cousin however many times removed, will turn up and have every right to put you out onto the street."

"I could find employment," Beatrix said with a sniff, reaching into her pocket to find a handkerchief. "I could be a governess, or a companion..."

Papa held out his hand. Beatrix gave up her search for a handkerchief and reached forward and took it, wishing she could hold on to him forever.

"You could. But I don't want you to be desperately trying to find paid work, worrying about whether you will have a roof over your head. I raised you as the daughter of an earl, and I do not want you to have to lower yourself in the world. Lord Filton may be older than you—"

"He's older than *you*, Papa."

"Yes. But he's not a cruel man, and he has a vast fortune, and an estate that you loved as a child..."

Beatrix nodded. She could see that her father only wanted what he thought was best for her. But it was hard to truly believe that marrying a man who was surely approaching five-and-sixty was the path to happiness for her.

"I won't push you into it. But I want you to seriously consider him. He would give you a safe future when I am no longer here."

It wasn't a topic that Beatrix wanted to discuss, but clearly her father was convinced that his death was in the not-too-distant future, so she needed to be prepared.

But it didn't need to be decided today. "Can we go to Bath for a little while? To take the waters...and to give me some time to think?" Beatrix pleaded. She couldn't imagine agreeing to wed the aging earl, and he surely wouldn't wait for an answer for long, considering how quickly he had started searching for a new wife after the death of the last Lady Filton.

"You know I would do anything to make you happy, my little bee."

Beatrix smiled through her tears; he hadn't called her that in a long time. Things were simple back when she had always been his little buzzing bee, and her mother had been alive, and no one would have even considered betrothing her to an old man.

Where had it all gone wrong?

"I'll instruct the staff to ready us to depart the day after to-morrow," Beatrix said, embracing her father. "The waters will work wonders—you'll see."

She would do anything to have more time with her beloved father. And on top of that, if her father's health was better, she wouldn't have to marry in such haste…

But marriage needed to be on the cards, and soon. There could be no more waiting around for cupid's arrow to strike.

"I just wished to inform you both that I shall be out of the city for a while," Spencer said, sipping his whisky in the quiet corner of the club that they had been frequenting of late.

Timothy frowned. "Are you heading to the countryside already? No one will be leaving the city for weeks yet."

It did not seem that Timothy understood Spencer's desire to be away from people—but he had no plans to go to the countryside. There were too many memories there.

"No. To Bath… I'll be back before the end of the Season."

"What can Bath offer that London cannot?" James asked, lighting a cigar.

Fewer people, for one. And no memories of his father or brother, since he had never visited the city with them. But he wasn't sure his friends would understand either of those.

And neither did he wish to share the real reason he had made the sudden decision to visit the spa town of Bath: to take the waters. He would have laughed at himself for such a notion a few years ago.

Did he really believe the waters could heal what ailed him? He wasn't convinced—but he wanted things to change. He wanted to be able to converse with his friends and young ladies like he had done before. He wanted to be able to sleep without waking screaming, haunted by the memories of what he had witnessed in France.

And people flocked to take the waters in Bath in order to cure themselves of all sorts of ills. Perhaps it would work for him, and he could return to being the man he once was.

"I just wish for a change of scenery."

He wasn't sure whether they believed him, but the next day his carriage was packed with his belongings and rattling its way to the city of Bath.

He chose to ride ahead, preferring to be saddle-sore than bored and stuck with his own thoughts in the carriage.

The light drizzle didn't bother him as his horse made good progress toward the inn he planned to stop at for the night. He could never completely escape his thoughts, but with the wind whistling in his ears and the rain spraying his face, he was at least distracted.

He was specifically trying not to think of Lady Beatrix. She was a temptation he knew he could not give into. She set something alight in him that he had thought was long dead. He wanted to see her smile. He wanted to talk to her. He wanted to press his lips to hers and pull her body close...

He was not doing a very good job of not thinking about her.

He barely knew her, and he wasn't sure why she was on his mind so much. And yet he found himself imagining what her golden hair would look like fanned out on his pillow, or how bright her blue eyes would look after he had kissed her senseless.

It was nice for his mind to wander to such a positive place, even if none of it could ever happen. He wasn't fit to be anyone's husband.

BATH WAS ALMOST as busy as London, although Spencer hoped he would not be recognized as he often was in the city. He was not known in Bath, and nor was his family; he would be quite happy if everyone he was acquainted with was busy enjoying the London Season, and he could be anonymous as he tried to find the Spencer he had been before the war.

He had brought his valet Allan, and the townhouse he had rented for his visit was equipped with a cook and a maid, but he did not require any more staff. After all, he was not planning on socializing or attending any functions, other than visiting the Pump Room to take the waters. At least in Bath, he would not need to worry about making a fool of himself in front of the beguiling Lady Beatrix.

CHAPTER EIGHT

I T HAD BEEN a long time since Beatrix had visited Bath, and it was busier than she remembered. The Pump Room was the place to be seen during the day, and many of the *ton* who were in Bath were promenading the great room even if they had no intention of taking the bitter waters, which rather unfortunately smelled like boiled eggs.

It had taken a day's rest after their journey for her father to feel well enough for the short walk from their Bath townhouse to the Pump Room, and he had grumbled the whole way there.

"I'm not sure waters can cure whatever ails me when doctors have failed."

"I know, Papa," Beatrix said for what seemed like the hundredth time. "But it is worth a try, is it not?"

And so they queued for the waters, and her father grimaced as he took them, and then they sat on marble benches and watched society for a little while. Society was well represented at the Pump Room, and Beatrix found it fascinating to sit in the great room and listen to the Pump Room band while watching young and old take the waters, promenade, or merely gossip.

Whilst Beatrix loved the excitement of London, she was relieved to have escaped—mainly due to the increasing attentions of Lord Filton. In spite of her father's concerns about what would happen to her if he passed away, she still could not bring herself to accept the man's suit. But she had never been very good at being bold or assertive, and he clearly took her reticence as mere shyness.

She would have to make her feelings clear once they returned to London, she knew that—no matter how hard she found the thought. But hopefully by then her father would be showing signs of improvement, and they could make a plan together to find her a suitable husband.

After all, she had a dowry, and she did not think she was unattractive. She had merely been forgotten, overlooked by eligible men in society. That could surely be remedied.

She was about to suggest they walk home for some luncheon when she saw *him*. Lord Leighton. Her eyes met his across the room and she could not help but gasp.

He was here. Her heart felt like it had stopped beating; there was no one in the room but her and Lord Leighton. Every time she told herself that she needed to forget him, that she would never see him again, he seemed to appear.

Like he was her destiny.

And yet, she had to remind herself, most of his actions suggested he had no interest in her. He had run away; he hadn't called on her; he had only been able to converse about the weather when they had met in the park.

But why did her body react in this way to him?

She had never felt such heat coursing through her body. Not even when her betrothed had kissed her. Nor when she had imagined being married to him.

Only when she was near Lord Leighton.

His gaze flicked to the door, and she wondered if he was about to flee.

"Lord Leighton!"

Beatrix jumped in surprise as her father called him over. She was amazed he recognized him across the room, and remembered his name. Her cheeks flushed as he made his way through the throng of well-dressed people toward them. She couldn't take her eyes off him. He was taller than most of the men in the room, and his dark hair was cut short.

Although she didn't think his waistcoat and jacket were the height of fashion now, as the style had been when she had met him seven years earlier, he still looked impeccably smart. Her gaze wandered to those full lips…but unlike in the past, they weren't pulled up in a smile. No, misery haunted his face, and she wondered what he had witnessed in his life to cast such a shadow across his visage. To take away the charming, vivacious young man and return a sullen, awkward marquess.

For the first time, she wondered if his attitude towards her wasn't actually due to something she had done.

He stopped before them and gave a sharp bow; Papa nodded his head, but did not stand. Beatrix did, and curtsied.

"Lord Haxbury, Lady Beatrix. A pleasure to see you in Bath."

"And you, Lord Leighton." Beatrix wanted to know if he'd taken the waters, and if so, why, but she could not just ask outright. And he did not seem to be one for sharing.

"I wish to sit a while longer, Bea," Papa said, leaning back in the wooden chair. "Why don't you and Lord Leighton promenade around the room while I regain my energy for our journey home."

"Oh. I—" Beatrix did not wish the Marquess to feel forced into walking with her, but she had to admit that she wanted to spend more time with him. Even if she wasn't sure whether he wanted to spend more time with her.

"It would be my pleasure," Lord Leighton said, holding out his arm for her to take.

The touch of his body against hers, even through her gloves, made her feel dizzy. She struggled to think of sensible things to say with him so close.

Why did he have this effect on her?

"Are you enjoying Bath?" he asked as they began a slow circuit of the room.

"Yes. I have not been in years…but I wanted my father to take the waters."

Lord Leighton nodded, and Beatrix wondered if that would be enough to prompt him to share his own reason for being there.

"Your father does not look like he enjoys the same good health that he used to."

Beatrix sighed. That was certainly true—and it broke her heart to think it was so noticeable to someone who barely knew him. "No. Age has not been kind to him. But we do not know exactly what ails him. So I hoped the waters…"

She looked up into his dark eyes, and smiled shyly. "I know it may sound silly. We have seen so many doctors, and some of them thought the waters might help, and some thought it was nonsense… But it's worth a try, is it not?"

His eyes crinkled as he smiled. "My thoughts exactly. And I fervently hope the waters help your father."

She was sure that he had taken the waters himself after that comment, but was still unsure why. "I hope you find them beneficial, too," she forced herself to say.

They did not speak for a moment, and Beatrix wondered if she had offended him. But then he said, "Thank you. I wish for nothing more." There was such conviction in his words that she felt like she was peeking through the armor he clearly wore around society. And yet she didn't feel she could ask what he was so desperate to cure. Perhaps it was something that could not be spoken about in company, or certainly in mixed company. She wouldn't want to embarrass him.

"Are you staying in Bath long?" she asked instead.

"I haven't decided. I find myself…unsure where I belong."

She did not know if the waters had loosened his tongue, or whether he just felt more free to express himself in Bath, but the conversation was most enlightening.

"I know how you feel." When he glanced down at her, she smiled warmly, her heart racing. Why would a marquess feel like he did not have a place? Beatrix's problem was slightly different: whilst she felt on the outskirts of society now as an unwed woman of five-and-twenty, she was fairly happy where she was, with her place by her father's side. But the fear of what would come after he passed, as much as she didn't want to think of it, darkened her heart and her thoughts more than she cared to admit, even to herself.

Unable to stop herself from speaking—or maybe because she wanted to get away from her gloomy musings by focusing on something positive, she said, "Will you be attending the ball at the Assembly Rooms on Wednesday night?" She had no idea what had made her so bold, other than that she was enjoying her conversation with him, and did not wish to leave it up to fate where and when they would meet again.

"I—" Lord Leighton did not seem sure of his answer. They completed an entire turn of the room and began another, without pausing. "I had not planned…"

"My father does not wish for me to miss out on society because we are here, so I shall be attending." Did she think that her attendance would sway him? *Foolish girl*, she warned herself as she hesitated in answering. *You are setting yourself up for a fall.*

"I do not frequent balls very often," he said slowly. "But I don't have any other plans while I'm in town. Perhaps you could save a dance for me…"

Beatrix's heart leapt and she could not control the smile that took over her face.

"Oh yes. I shall."

CHAPTER NINE

S PENCER DIDN'T KNOW what he had been thinking, saying yes to attending a public ball at the Assembly Rooms. One of the reasons he had come to Bath was to get away from society's expectations—and now he had asked Lady Beatrix to save him a dance.

Yet, there was something about her that made it impossible for him to think sensibly. So many times he wished that he had never gone to war—or more precisely, that Jack had never signed up, and therefore he had not followed his big brother. Because in that scenario, his brother would still be alive, and everything would be as it was.

But there was no way to turn back time, and he had come to terms with the fact that he was now the Marquess of Leighton, and that his life would never be like it was before.

He'd thought that locking himself away from the world was the answer—but that didn't seem to work. And neither did he wish to attend society's functions and make a fool of himself running away every time someone dropped a glass or set off fireworks.

And although it made no sense, and he didn't really know what to say to her, and seeing her often put him in situations he'd been trying to avoid, he did want to see more of Lady Beatrix. Perhaps, he mused, familiarity would bring resolution.

So maybe…if he could fix himself, if the waters worked, if a doctor could come up with some remedy to the night terrors and the overreaction to loud noises and the horrors that haunted him…then maybe he could have a future.

A future with Lady Beatrix.

Once upon a time, he had imagined her as his wife. It was a time when he did not think much of marriage, and the dream had seemed so far in the future. But she was the only woman he had ever considered marrying, and she was the only woman he had smiled around since he had been home.

The only woman—the only person—whom he had told that he did not know his place in the world. Amazingly she hadn't responded with the disdain he'd expected, nor with contempt, or any of the various feelings he had already heaped upon himself. "I know how you feel," she had said.

How could that be, he wondered. Was she just being polite? That was a possibility, but deep in his heart, he thought there was more to what she'd said than just niceties.

Still, she didn't deserve to be tied to a broken man. He didn't understand why she was not yet wed; it wasn't something he could just ask her, either. That would be presuming far too much.

So he would go to the ball, and dance with her, and hope he could find a way to fix himself so that he didn't have to fight the temptation to see her, to take her hand, to kiss her…

⸎

IT HAD BEEN a long time since Lady Beatrix Chichester had felt excited about a ball. When she had first come out in society, each ball had been the highlight of her week. Even after the disappointment of the then-Lord Clement not calling on her, she had still been thrilled to dress up and accompany her father to the balls thrown by the highest in society.

She had accepted every dance opportunity and thrilled at getting to show off the skills she had honed, thanks to years with a dance tutor.

It had still been exciting in her second Season. She loved to see the way the ballrooms were decorated, to marvel at the inventive ways society found to stand out from the common crowd. Papa had never hosted a ball—with Mama gone, he never seemed to have the desire. He never did remarry, and so there was no new Lady Haxbury to take her mother's place in society. Still, he'd dutifully escorted her to every single one, and right up until Ambrose's death, in that foolish duel, Beatrix had looked forward to them.

But once she was out of mourning, they became a chore. She had been forgotten by society, a wallflower disappearing into the fringes, rarely asked to dance, rarely even noticed.

With her father's worsening health, it was not difficult to start declining the majority of the invitations.

And yet on that Wednesday night in Bath, as Jemima helped her to dress for the ball at the Assembly Rooms, excitement filled her stomach.

Lord Leighton had asked her to save him a dance.

Surely that suggested that he had some interest in her? She did not want to start picturing a wedding, not when she had so foolishly daydreamed about this man for so many years... But it had to mean something, surely, that he wanted to attend the ball when he usually did not, and that he had specifically said he would dance with her.

They arrived at the Assembly Rooms early. Beatrix had been too excited to wait around once she was ready, and when they entered, there was only a handful of people milling around. None of them were Lord Leighton.

Ever the optimist, she hid her disappointment and told herself it was early. She settled her father in a chair with a drink and sat beside him to watch the door like a hawk.

When the ballroom was full to bursting with the rich and important of Bath society, Beatrix began to wonder whether he truly was coming. She watched couples take to the dance floor—

mainly young men and women who looked to be entering into courtship, but sometimes couples who were already married, or widows and widowers finding a second or even third chance at happiness.

Her heart sank lower with the start of every dance as her disappointment grew. He had said he would call on her once before and had never appeared. Instead, he'd gone to war. Then he had run away at Vauxhall Gardens, and then, promptly departed St James's Park.

Had she been foolish to expect him to come? She thought things would be different here. And it was true that he seemed more at ease with her in the Pump Rooms. But perhaps that had all been a façade. Or a mistake, which now he realized he was keen to rectify by staying away from her …

❁

"MILORD, IF YOU do not wish to be late…"

"Thank you, Allan." Spencer sat back in his armchair, downed a glass of whisky, and poured another one. His valet was right; if he was going to actually attend this ball, as he had said he would, he needed to leave.

He hadn't been forced into agreeing to attend. All it had taken was a pretty young lady asking if he would attend, and he had said "yes".

Asked her to save a dance, even.

And yet here he was, sitting in the library drinking whisky, unable to force himself out of the door.

Why had he agreed to go? She'd be expecting him, and he did not want to let her down again. But the thought of a packed ballroom, eyes on him, the risk of someone realizing how broken he really was…

It didn't help that he'd been plagued with nightmares the previous night. Worse than usual, too; these had started as they usually did, with him in France, his musket pointed at some helpless Frenchman, the smell of gunpowder, the pounding of cannons, the boom of musket fire, and the whizzing sound of musket balls flying through the air. The feeling of the ground rocking beneath his feet with each concussion, and the screams.

And then he pressed the trigger, and it wasn't just a nameless, faceless Frenchman who was lying dead before him. No, it was Jack, his beloved older brother, dead in the grass at his feet and by Spencer's own hand. As real as if it had really happened that way, even though it had not.

He had awoken in a cold sweat. He was sure he'd been shouting out, too, but his valet knew by now not to disturb him. When he'd first come home, Allan had run in every time…but there was no need. No point. No one could help him.

He had struggled to get back to sleep, the image of Jack, dead, filling his mind whenever he closed his eyes—and now here he was, tired and irritable and two glasses of whisky down, trying to decide if he really ought to attend the ball.

"You're being pathetic," he told himself. "Pull yourself together."

But his mind rallied back: *Maybe you're doing her a favor.*

He wanted to be whole again. And he had no idea how he was going to achieve that. The waters certainly hadn't dispelled the nightmares, even though he had drunk them every day. There hadn't been a loud noise to test his nerves as of yet, but he didn't feel any different. Other than the fact that he wanted to see Lady Beatrix, and dance with her again, and be the one to make her smile.

And so he forced himself out of his chair, finished his drink and strode to the doorway, calling out that he was leaving to a surprised Allan as he did so.

CHAPTER TEN

T HE BALL WAS in full swing when he arrived, and when he entered he was accosted by the warmth of so many bodies in a room together and the level of noise from the musicians and the attendees.

He forced himself to walk through the crowd, even though a large part of him wanted to walk away. He was already late. There was a chance she had already left. But just in case... His eyes scanned the dance floor to see if he could spot her amongst the couples there, but there was no sign of her golden hair.

He walked the perimeter, smiling politely when he caught the eye of any of the young ladies looking to dance, but not stopping.

He was only here to dance with one lady.

And just when he thought that she must have left, that he'd messed up yet again, he spotted her. She was standing next to her father, who was seated on a chair looking rather disinterested. She was watching the dancers, which Spencer thought was a crying shame—she should be dancing.

With him.

He cut through the crowd, not allowing his anxieties to get the better of him, and stopped right in front of them.

Lady Beatrix's eyes widened when she realized it was he, and he beamed in response, his heart lifting in spite of his recent reticence. "Good evening, Lady Beatrix, Lord Haxbury. I apologize. I realize I am rather tardy to the dance tonight."

"Indeed you are," Lord Haxbury said, and Spencer thought he heard a hint of disapproval. "We were planning to leave soon."

Lady Beatrix bit her full, pink bottom lip, making it plump and grow more rosy, and Spencer found it hard to focus on his next question. "My apologies. I was hoping you would still have a dance free, Lady Beatrix…"

Her answering smile warmed his heart. How had he been thinking that he might not come tonight? And why were these other men so foolish that they did not ask this gem of a woman to dance?

She glanced at her father, hope in her eyes. "Would you mind awfully if we stayed for one more dance, Papa?"

For a moment, Spencer thought her father might refuse. But it seemed he, too, loved to see his daughter smile.

"Of course. Take as long as you like. I'll be here when you're ready."

⟫⟪

BEATRIX HATED HERSELF for being so pleased to see Lord Leighton, and for appearing so desperate to dance.

But she couldn't help it. She could not hide her excitement. She had been waiting for him, and she had thought that he would not come.

And now here he was. Oh, she knew it was only one dance. But she had been so disappointed in her many years out in society that she was rather too easily pleased.

He looked more handsome than ever. His cheeks were red, his eyes bright, and she no longer cared that he had missed most of the ball.

After all, he was here now. And he wanted to dance with her.

There was a shortage of men at the ball, and he could have had his pick of young ladies. Indeed, Beatrix had only been asked to dance once all night, before Lord Leighton had appeared. And she had chosen her prettiest pale pink dress for the occasion and had Jemima plait her hair so that it looked like a crown.

And still, she went unnoticed.

"Shall we, Lady Beatrix?" Lord Leighton said, and she took his offered hand and felt like this was where she belonged.

The dance was one she knew very well, and it seemed Lord Leighton did too, for he did not trip up as he had done when they had danced at Vauxhall Gardens.

He made her feel tongue-tied, but she could not turn down the opportunity to speak with him. For who knew when she would next get the chance?

"I thought you might not be attending after all," she said, unintentionally admitting how much she had thought about the situation.

Lord Leighton closed his eyes momentarily. "I must apologize. I find social situations…somewhat challenging."

What on earth did that mean? That he wished to live in the country like Lord Filton? She thought she remembered him saying that he did not wish to return to the country… And yet, she found herself thinking that she would not mind being secluded in the countryside so much if it was with Lord Leighton.

Foolish girl. Don't get ahead of yourself. You are not living in a fairy tale.

"Well, I'm glad that you came," she told him honestly. For what was the point in hiding how she felt? She was sure she had already come across as a pathetic spinster. No point in turning back now.

"I'm glad I did too," he said with a smile that nearly stopped her heart. "And I hope it is not too forward of me to tell you how beautiful you look tonight."

She felt her cheeks flaming red and looked down at the floor, missing a step. She could not remember the last time she had been so complimented. Well, Lord Filton had tried to compliment her, but when he spoke the words made her feel uncomfortable.

Lord Leighton's words made her feel like she might burst into flames on the spot.

"Thank you..." She looked into his dark eyes and felt as though they were the only two people in the room. This was what she had always dreamed about. Romance, a love match, feeling giddy at the thought of seeing someone. And she had thought that she had lost the chance for such a thing to happen to her when he had not called on her, and then when Ambrose had died. But perhaps she still had a chance...

"Would your father forgive me if I asked for another dance, do you think? Of course, unless you are otherwise engaged..."

He surely knew that she had no dances lined up—she had been standing with the wallflowers watching the dancing when he had arrived, not in the fray. But she appreciated him asking anyway. People would surely talk if they danced together twice in a row...but she found she didn't care.

She wanted to dance with him.

"I think he'll forgive you," she said with a smile. "But then I will have to take him home before he falls asleep in his chair."

The second dance was more complicated, but in spite of how rarely she danced these days, Beatrix still remembered every step. Every time her eyes met Lord Leighton's, she found herself blushing, and she barely noticed when he missed a step or almost caught her toes beneath his boots.

It was another magical evening, one she'd had precious few of in her life, and she knew she would remember it forever.

The musicians reached the crescendo of the piece when there was a sudden crash. Beatrix whirled around to see an inebriated-looking man surrounded by broken glasses; by the looks of the very wet floor and the silver tray rolling away, he had knocked into someone carrying a large number of drinks.

As the staff hurried in to clean up, Beatrix turned back to Lord Leighton—to find him ashen-faced and frozen to the spot.

"Lord Leighton?"

"I—excuse me." He barely got the words out before he dashed from the floor, leaving Beatrix alone in the chaos.

For a moment, Beatrix stood where she had been left, unsure what to do. She didn't think anyone had noticed him departing so abruptly, thanks to the smashed glass... She wanted to follow him, to see if he was all right, to find out what had happened to make him run away. Because this time, she was sure she hadn't done anything to prompt his exit.

She glanced over at her father, and saw—in spite of the loud crash—he had indeed fallen asleep in his chair. And so, without thinking any further, she turned on her heel and followed Lord Leighton from the ballroom.

CHAPTER ELEVEN

W*HY, WHY, WHY did you come?* Spencer asked himself as he tried to dispel the sound of guns from his mind in the small, and thankfully empty, card room he had secreted himself in.

He wasn't ready to be out in society. He'd made a fool of himself yet again, and Lady Beatrix, too—which was the last thing he wanted.

He hoped she would go home with her father and forget all about him. Because there was no way he was going to subject her to such behavior again.

Even though the tap on the door was quiet, it made him jump. His nerves were far too fragile after the crash of the glasses. And then the door opened, and he froze in the darkness. The moonlight through the window was enough to allow him to see who was in the doorway, and his heart raced even faster.

Lady Beatrix paused, blinked rapidly, and then stepped into the card room.

"I'm sorry," Spencer said hurriedly. "I shouldn't—"

"I just wanted to check that you were well. And see what was wrong…"

Spencer shook his head. He couldn't explain what was wrong. And she shouldn't be here in a dark room alone with him.

"You should go. I'll… I'll call on you. I just need…"

She took a few, slow steps toward him, surprisingly bold.

"You told me you'd call on me before."

Shame filled his chest. "I'm sorry. I—"

And then she was close enough to reach out and take his hand. He knew he should send her away, get himself together and leave this place and her entirely. But it was so comforting to have her warm hand around his that he couldn't bring himself to.

"What happened, Lord Leighton?" she asked softly.

"Don't call me that."

Her eyes widened at his abrupt rebuttal.

"Please…"

She swallowed. "What should I call you?"

He looked out of the window, unable to handle the confusion in her eyes. What *could* she call him? He wasn't Lord Clement anymore, as much as he wished he was. "I shouldn't be Lord Leighton," he muttered, more to himself than her.

"Very well." She spoke to him as though he were a frightened animal that might bolt at any moment, and with how shaken he felt after the crashing of the glasses, he thought it wasn't a bad assessment.

He wanted her to call him Spencer. But it wouldn't be right.

"Why did you run?"

"The glasses…" He swallowed, his mouth dry, as now she encased his hand between both of hers. "Loud noises. I always think…" He trailed off, embarrassed to admit the truth, but she didn't interrupt, and she didn't leave, and after some deep breaths and hard swallows, he told her. "In my head, they're guns. I know it makes no sense. But it brings everything back…"

She rubbed a soothing thumb across his hand and the motion sent shivers down his spine. "Ah. So the fireworks…"

He nodded. "The war broke me. I'm sorry. I should not have pursued you. And I should not be here with you. I—"

"I don't think you're broken," Beatrix murmured, holding his hand tightly in hers. She was glad to have some understanding, even though it made her heart ache to think of him, so afflicted. The horrors he must have seen…

"Jumping at loud noises is only part of it," he said, giving her a sad smile. "I'm not who I was before, and no matter how hard I try to get back to that man I was seven years ago in Vauxhall Gardens, I'm not him."

"None of us are who we were seven years ago," Beatrix said, squeezing his hand. "I was seventeen and believed in the joy and magic the world was going to offer me. But I don't, anymore."

"You should still believe in joy and magic," Spencer said sadly.

"Do you?"

The look he gave her was so devastating that tears welled up in her eyes; one escaped and made a cold trail down her cheek. He reached with the thumb of his free hand to swipe the lone tear away, and Beatrix felt her breath hitch.

It was a moment of sadness and honesty and heartbreak, and yet his touch made her whole body come alive.

He thought he was broken. But she didn't care. She needed him. She didn't know why or how, but she knew that *this* was the man she wanted. The man she was meant for.

She stood on tiptoes, and he leaned toward her, and they were close enough that she could feel his warm breath on her skin. Hands still clasped, Beatrix thought her heart might beat right out of her chest. If someone walked in right now she would be ruined—but she couldn't find it in herself to care.

And then the music started up again, and Spencer jumped away from her.

"I must go. I'm sorry." He ripped his hand out of hers and was gone from the room before she could argue with him.

And she knew, as she escorted her father home, that she would definitely remember this night for the rest of her life. Not for its magical qualities but for the fact that she had thought everything she had ever wanted was finally in her grasp—and then it had been torn cruelly away.

BEATRIX DIDN'T SEE Lord Leighton again in Bath, and when she and her father returned to London, she regretted ever going. The waters had not had the desired effect. In fact, all the travel only seemed to have made her father more tired and more prone to his fits of breathlessness. She was at a loss as to what else she could do for him.

The only benefit to her absence was that upon returning to London, she soon discovered that Lord Filton had proposed marriage to another young woman.

Even though her prospects were worse than when she left London, and even though she felt rather heartbroken at the dream she'd had of a romance between herself and Lord Leighton being cruelly torn away, she was overwhelmed with relief. No matter what her life held in store for her, she did not want to be wed to the elderly earl.

"Do you have any plans today, my little bee?" Papa asked with a kindly smile one morning as the Season drew to a close. Normally, they would be thinking about returning to the countryside, like the rest of the *ton*—but she was worried that such travel would only make her father more ill.

She shook her head. "No plans, Papa. Would you like to take a walk? It's a pleasant day."

Her father shook his head. "I think I'm too tired today. But you should go out, get some fresh air. You shouldn't be locked away with an old man like me."

She reached out and took his hand. "You know I'm quite happy to sit with you. I have needlework to do, and some correspondence to catch up on."

"No. I think I will go for a rest, so that I have more energy for conversation at dinner. You go for a walk, enjoy the sunshine—it will only be a few short months until all we see is rain."

"If you're sure…" Beatrix helped her father to stand. He embraced her, and she was rather surprised at such an unprompted display of affection.

"Enjoy the sunshine, my love. For you have been the light of my life—and I don't wish yours to be dark because I have grown weary with age."

Had she known that she would never speak with her father again, there were so many things she would have said. But alas, she simply watched him slowly mount the stairs to bed.

CHAPTER TWELVE

EVEN THOUGH IT was clear that the waters were not helping his affliction at all, Spencer stayed in Bath for a few more weeks before returning to London. He was filled with embarrassment and frustration at the scene he had caused at the Assembly Rooms. Ducking when the glasses were dropped, running from the room, and then the moment with Lady Beatrix in the abandoned card room which should not have happened…

And yet part of him hoped to see her wandering the streets of Bath. Even though he knew that he was being foolish. She had come to check on him in that small, dark room, and held his hand, and she could have been ruined for doing so.

There had been a moment when he had thought he could fix himself, and pursue Lady Beatrix. But the incident at the Assembly Rooms had made it clear that if he possibly could overcome his destroyed nerves, it would not be for a long time. And he would not destroy Lady Beatrix's reputation—especially when he was in no position to offer marriage.

By the time he returned to London, sick of the waters and with no idea what he was going to do once the Season ended, the early summer sunshine was already filling the sky. He traveled by horse again, his belongings following in the carriage, and when he reached his London townhouse, his skin was bronzed more than current fashions would approve.

Not that he cared. If people wanted to gossip about him,

there were far worse things they could say than that he had stayed out in the sun a little too long.

On the off chance that they would be there, Spencer decided to go to the club on his first night back, to let Timothy and James know that he had returned. They had surely been wrapped up in the social events of the Season, and barely noticed his absence—but it only seemed right to inform them that he was now home.

If this was his home… Was he to stay in London permanently, even when the fashionable set left for their country estates? Or could he bear to return to his own seat, and live the life that should have been Jack's? Perhaps he could choose another of the houses belonging to him to settle in. One with no memories…

He was surprised at how pleased he was to see his friends at their usual corner table. He had come early, hoping to catch them before whatever ball or musicale they were attending that night, but he hadn't expected to find he had missed their company so very much.

He still wasn't sure how to behave in any company, but it had been lonely in Bath. He didn't want to always be alone, even though his mind plagued him, and socializing did not feel natural any longer.

"Leighton!" Timothy called out, raising his glass in welcome. "You've returned!"

Spencer signaled that he wished for a glass to join his friends in the decanter of port they were enjoying before taking a seat. "I am. And pleased to be so."

James beamed. "Good. Did Bath offer everything you hoped?"

Spencer took a sip of his drink in order to think of an answer. "I saw Lady Beatrix, while I was there," he said, in order to avoid discussing his taking of the waters, and their lack of effectiveness.

Knowing glances passed between Timothy and James. "Did you indeed. And was that the reason you went?"

"No, but—"

"It's even more sad, if she only just got home from her travels. Was her father with her in Bath?" Timothy asked.

"Yes, he was. What's sad?"

"Well, unless I've heard wrong… At the races today, the talk was all of how Lord Haxbury had been found dead, by his daughter no less."

"What?" Spencer's mouth dropped open in shock and he nearly spilled the ruby-red liquid across his lap. "What do you mean? I saw the man only a fortnight ago…"

He had looked rather feeble, it was true. But surely not at death's door?

"Perhaps I heard wrong," Timothy said, although Spencer could tell he was merely trying to placate him. "Or it was a lord with a similar sounding name."

"I was sure I heard them mention Lady Beatrix by name, though," James chimed in.

Spencer felt like he might be sick. She would be heartbroken. She doted upon her father, and had hoped so much that the waters would cure him. If he had truly passed shortly after they had returned home…

He glanced up at the clock. It was far too late for it to be acceptable to call upon her. And there wasn't anything he could do… But he wanted to be there for her. To offer his condolences. He knew the pain of grief better than most.

BEATRIX WAS IN shock. She sat alone in the parlor, the drapes still drawn, feeling uncomfortable in her ill-fitting black dress. How could everything change so suddenly? One moment she had been enjoying the early summer sunshine, and the next she had returned home, and checked upon her father, and discovered…

The doctor said his heart must have given out. She'd known for a long time that he was ill and weak, but she had not truly expected him to suddenly leave her. In the blink of an eye her world was turned upside down, and there she was, seven days after the awful discovery, wearing the dress that she had not worn since Ambrose had been killed in that duel, and trying to see how to escape from this misery.

The house seemed so quiet and empty without him. The grief was overwhelming. She could not sleep, could not eat, could not think of anything but her dear papa, and how she had not been there in his final moments on this earth.

Why had she gone on that walk?

Why had she dragged him to Bath? Yes, she had hoped that the waters would help him. But it was also for her own selfish reason: to escape the odious Lord Filton, because she still had dreams of a love match.

She hated herself for hastening her father's end with so much travel.

Although she felt alone, she was not entirely. The staff continued as they normally did, making meals that Beatrix could not eat, and clearing them away untouched. Jemima, her dear maid, had taken to checking in on her every hour, and so when there was a knock on the parlor door, she presumed that was who it was.

"All is well, Jemima," she called out, her voice sounding hollow. She loved her maid for caring so much, but she just didn't have any conversation in her.

"Sorry, milady," a male voice said, pushing the door open. "It's not Jemima." Beatrix looked up to see the awkward expression on the face of their butler, Samson, at the door. "You have a visitor, milady."

Beatrix shook her head, her eyes welling with tears at the thought of having to speak to anyone. "I cannot, Samson. I am in mourning, please tell whoever it is—"

"He's very insistent. Says you must admit him…"

Beatrix pressed her eyes closed momentarily to keep the tears at bay and stood. She was the lady of the house, after all—well, she would be until the heir came to take it all away. But that was a thought for another day.

Chapter Thirteen

UNABLE TO UNDERSTAND why anyone would insist on being admitted to a house so recently bereaved, Beatrix shook her head. "I will inform whoever is trying to barge in to a home in mourning that it is not a suitable time." She swept from the room, her misery fueling her anger.

The man on the doorstep was not one whom she recognized. He was tall, with ashen blond hair and blue eyes that were a little too small for his face. He looked at least ten years her senior, if not more, and she drew herself up to her full height to inform him she did not wish to have any visitors.

"Lady Beatrix," he said, with a bow. "I am so sorry for your loss."

"Thank you." She did not bother to enquire his name. "I am afraid I am in mourning, as you are aware, and shall not be entertaining guests at the time. So good day."

And she was going to turn and allow Samson to close the door in the rude stranger's face—until he laughed.

"I am afraid there's been a misunderstanding, Lady Beatrix. I am here to take my rightful place, as Lord Haxbury."

Beatrix's blood ran cold. That name should not belong to any other than her father. And she had thought she would have time before the new heir, some distant cousin of her father's, came knocking. Of course, a letter had been sent upon her father's death, but that had been mere days earlier. She had not thought he would arrive so soon, or be quite so keen to take his place in society…

She swallowed, forcing back more tears, and made herself curtsy. She would be polite to this man. She had to be—he was the only one with any power to make sure she did not end up on the streets. She had no brothers, no uncles, no one to take her in. She had not married, as her father had advised, in order to protect herself in this ghastly situation.

She was alone in this world, and this man had everything that had once been hers.

"Lord Haxbury," she said, the words sticking in her throat. "My apologies. I was not expecting you. Please, come in."

It felt odd to welcome him into the home that technically belonged to him. Most of her father's wealth and properties passed on with his title to his heir—and that, of course, could not be her, a mere woman.

"Samson. We'll take some tea in the drawing room, please."

In the week since she'd lost her father, Beatrix felt like she'd forgotten how to make conversation. Her heart ached too terribly for what she had lost, and when she thought of the future, it terrified her. How could she make small talk in the wake of such pain?

"Allow me to say again how sorry I am for your loss. I hear your father was a fine man."

Beatrix smiled with watery eyes. "He was. Did you ever meet him?"

"Alas, I did not get the chance. The family link between us is quite distant—I just happen to be the only other male on this side of the family." His snake-like smile made her feel a little queasy. There was something about him she did not like, but she told herself it was just the grief talking. She wouldn't have liked anyone who came in to take her father's place and her childhood homes.

"Indeed. It is a strange system of inheritance we have in this country."

Lord Haxbury pursed his lips, but the arrival of the tea stopped him from saying anything in response.

"Will there be anything else, milady?" the footman asked Beatrix.

"I—" she began, but then looked to Lord Haxbury. "Will you be staying, my lord? I have not made any arrangements for myself yet, I am afraid to say…"

He waved a hand in the air dismissively. "Do not worry, my dear. There is time to sort all of that. But yes, I will stay."

"A room made up then, for… Lord Haxbury."

The footman's eyes widened. "Yes, milady. Milord."

It was his house. Of course he could stay. And yet it wasn't really appropriate for them to be under the same roof with no other female of their class present… She would have to make a plan soon, if she did not wish for her reputation to be besmirched.

She hoped the staff would not make up her father's room for this new lord. Of course, it was his by rights—but she could not cope with the idea of someone else in it just yet. She had not even had a chance to sort through his belongings—the personal ones of no value, that she would surely be allowed to keep.

They were left alone to sip tea in an awkward atmosphere, and Beatrix tried to focus on being polite, when all she wanted to do was retreat to her chamber and hide from the world.

"Did it take you long to reach London?" she asked, trying to remember where the solicitor had said he was sending the missive to the new heir.

"I was actually already on my way, to see some friends at the end of the Season," he said with a toothy smile. "And then they had invited me on to a house party. Naturally, I shall no longer be attending—there is much to be done. I was rather surprised when my stable lad came riding at full speed from my home, to inform me an important letter had arrived."

"I can imagine." It was hard for Beatrix to comprehend how the worst event in her life could be the best in someone else's.

This gentleman—whose name she didn't even remember,

beyond the fact that he was now Lord Haxbury—clearly had plans now that he was an earl.

Plans that she was sure would not include the spinster daughter of the old earl. She needed to make a plan of her own, and fast.

"I would be happy to go through the accounts with you, if it would help. Alongside my father's man of business, I helped to run the estates while my father was ill."

He had been ill for so long, and yet she had always thought he would recover. She'd never truly imagined being alone in the world, both her parents gone, with no one to support her.

"How wonderful," Lord Haxbury said, in a tone that was laced with sarcasm. "Thank you, but I am sure I can go through everything with Mr. Mellor myself, without needing to take any of your time."

Feeling thoroughly put in her place, Beatrix sipped her tea and tried not to let her irritation show on her face.

"I need to make a plan, for my future," she said, preempting any thoughts he might have of when she would move on. "I hope you can allow me to stay until I have accommodation secured." She thought she was better to presume he would be generous, rather than asking if she could stay.

She had some jewelry she could probably sell, and a little pin money saved up—but aside from that, nothing to pay for her keep. Becoming a paid companion or a governess seemed like her only option, even though her father had been quite against the idea.

She wanted to cry whenever she thought of him, but that would do no good. He was gone, and she had not married when he had suggested it, so now she was alone in the world.

"Of course, my dear," he said, with a generous, if patronizing, wave of his hand through the air. "As I said, plenty of time to worry about the details. I have some thoughts about your future, if you are willing to entertain them."

Her smile was tight and forced. This man was taking everything she had ever known, and now he thought he could direct her future? She was not under his guardianship; she was a grown woman of twenty-five, and while she could not inherit an earldom or the fortune that came with it, she could make her own decisions about where her life would take her.

If only she had some viable options. "I would of course be interested in your thoughts, my lord."

"We will discuss it tomorrow, once I've had some time to settle in," he said, and she knew she would be anxious about whatever it was he had to say until that time. She needed to get copies of any magazines that carried advertisements, and find out what paid positions there were for a titled lady with nothing.

Unbidden, her thoughts flitted to Lord Leighton. She had not heard from him since she had returned from Bath, nor since her father's death. She doubted she would ever see him again. And yet his handsome face came to her mind—even though he could not help her in this situation. The best option, clearly, was for her to wed... But she could not wholly give up on wanting to marry someone she loved. Or at least held in high regard. She did not want some ancient earl... But it had been a long time since anyone else had offered.

She was well and truly on the shelf.

CHAPTER FOURTEEN

S PENCER SPENT SEVERAL days trying to decide whether he ought to call on Lady Beatrix to offer his condolences.

His first instinct was to do so. The few times they had met, they had always spoken, and in Bath, she had been more understanding than he could have expected. Yes, he didn't think he ought to pursue his romantic feeling towards her, but that didn't mean he couldn't express how sorry he was for the loss of her father, did it?

But he had never called on her. And in the cold light of day, the prospect was rather daunting. What if she read something into it—something he could not follow through on? Or, worse, what if she slammed the door in his face after his strange behavior every time they had met?

And so it was eight days after he had returned to London, and nine since her father had died, that he told himself to stop being such a coward. He liked to think he was a good man, raised with principles and honor, and such things surely necessitated that he inform Lady Beatrix of how sorry he was for her loss.

He did not tell his friends of his plan. They would surely read too much into it, too—especially as he did not make a habit of calling on young ladies. He hadn't before he'd gone to France, either... But that was because he was having far too much fun to have anyone thinking he was marking them out as his future wife.

Now he did not believe he would have a future wife.

BEATRIX HATED COMING downstairs to find the new heir—whose Christian name she had rifled through her father's documents to find—seated at the head of the table, breaking his fast and looking like he owned the place.

Which, of course, he did.

Even though she now knew his first name was Thomas, she could not imagine ever using it out loud. She didn't plan to be in this house long enough that he would ask her to use his first name. It was too awkward—and that was ignoring the damage that would be done to her reputation once the *ton* knew that they were living under the same roof, unchaperoned.

And yet she would surely be the topic of gossip once she found herself a paid position somewhere. There was no positive side to either solution.

He stood when she entered, and it hurt her heart to see Papa's place taken. She was pleased, however, that her new black dress had arrived from the dressmaker's the previous afternoon. At least she could greet the intruder feeling confident that she looked every part the lady that she was.

"Good morning, Lady Beatrix."

"Good morning, Lord Haxbury," she said, taking her seat and selecting a pastry from the plate in the center of the table. She did not really have an appetite, but she thought she should at least try.

"I trust you slept well?" Thomas said, taking a second pastry.

"Yes, thank you," Beatrix lied. She had barely slept since her father had died—and the bags under her eyes were surely apparent to anyone who bothered to look. "And you?"

"Oh yes. After so much traveling, I was ready to take to my bed."

Beatrix was sure the decanter of port she had seen him polishing off had also helped matters, but she did not say so.

"Do you have any plans for today?" she asked, time seeming to tick by incredibly slowly. It wasn't that there was anything particularly wrong with the man, she thought—just that she resented his intrusion on her grief.

Well, and he was rather patronizing. But perhaps she was judging him too quickly.

"I plan to look at the accounts, and get all the properties sorted in my head, before I decide where I am to live."

She nodded, but found she could not say anything. Those properties were the homes she had grown up in, spent her summers in, places where she had fond memories with her mother and father.

And now they were no longer hers. She could not stay in them, she would not make memories in them. Of course, she had always known that, as a girl, they would never be hers. That she would marry one day, and her husband's home would become hers. But that didn't make the reality any easier to bear.

"And you, Lady Beatrix?"

Of course he was asking her the same question, and yet she found she did not have an answer. She could no longer wallow in misery in the parlor undisturbed, for he was there now.

"I…might go for a walk. I have not decided."

"Would you have time to come and speak with me in the study? I have a matter I wish to discuss with you."

"Of course, my lord." Anxiety bubbled in her stomach. She had a bad feeling about whatever it was he wanted to suggest to her.

And she was right to feel that way.

An hour after breakfast, when she had decided she would go and get some fresh air, with her maid Jemima for company, she passed by the study door. With the door closed, it was easy to imagine that Papa was still behind it, reading some ancient myth that he'd newly discovered, or attending to the accounts.

But he was not, and the man who was behind the door wished to speak with her—and she thought she'd better get it over with before her walk.

She knocked, and the strange voice called "enter" and she felt goosebumps prickling across her arms at the horrible situation in which she found herself.

"Ah, Lady Beatrix. Please, take a seat."

This is my home! she wanted to scream. *I have come to this house every Season for my entire life. It is not your place to order me around.*

But she kept her mouth shut. Because she knew that, legally, he was perfectly entitled to be sitting in her father's chair, rifling through his carefully ordered paperwork.

Still, it didn't feel right.

"I have a proposition for you."

She sat before him, folded her hands in her lap, and waited to hear what he had to say.

"I understand that you did not expect your father's sudden death, and have no other family, or plans for your future."

Was he about to kick her out?

"No, I don't, but—"

He gave her a strained smiled and held up his hand to silence her. "Please, Lady Beatrix, if you'll allow me to finish. I have unexpectedly found myself as an earl, with estates and money I had not envisioned I would ever have—or if I did, not for many more years."

Beatrix was unsure how old he was; thirty-five or older, she thought, perhaps approaching forty. She didn't even know how long he had been Papa's heir; it wasn't something they had ever talked about. She presumed he had a father he had lost in order for him to be in this position. Perhaps brothers and uncles, too.

"And a man in my position needs a suitable wife. A woman of good breeding, who knows how to behave, and can provide handsome, intelligent heirs."

His frank talk surprised her. He was clearly keen to wed and move a wife in as soon as possible—and a new countess surely would not want the old earl's daughter around.

Not that she wanted to stay. Well, she did—but not with him there. And that was not possible.

"And so I rather think the solution to both our problems is that we wed."

Beatrix was sure she had misheard him. Her mouth dropped open, and he surely thought she was a simpleton, for he had to call her name several times before she managed to respond.

"You mean—"

"I think you should become my wife, yes. You could keep everything your father worked for, and I would have a suitable wife who knows what it takes to be a countess."

"I—I—" She couldn't get a thought out, even if she had known *what* it was that she thought.

"You will need some time to think, of course. Perhaps you could give me your answer by the end of the week? If you are not amenable to the suggestion, I would like to begin searching for other candidates as soon as possible."

She left the room in a daze. It was the most unexpected proposal of marriage she had ever received—and the most unromantic. And yet…he was offering for her to keep her home, her possessions, her position, her staff…

As unromantic and distasteful as she found him, the notion could not be dismissed out of hand.

CHAPTER FIFTEEN

H E NEARLY TURNED around and walked home several times, before telling himself to stop being so ridiculous. He had thought he would never see Lady Beatrix again—even if he had hoped otherwise, unwisely—and now he was stood on her doorstep, feeling nervous about knocking.

He forced himself to do so and when the butler opened the door, a black armband around his upper right arm, he asked, "Is Lady Beatrix at home to visitors?"

"I will check, my lord. And you are—"

"Lord Leighton. I am aware the house is in mourning, I merely wish to offer my condolences."

The butler bowed his head. "Very good, my lord. If you will please wait here a moment."

After wondering whether he ought to have come, Spencer wondered if she would see him. Perhaps she would refuse because of their awkward parting the last time they met... Did she know how close he had come to kissing her, alone in that card room?

If she did, she would surely send him away, appalled at his behavior.

Or perhaps she would refuse to see him because she was in mourning. He certainly would not have been capable of sitting and making polite conversation after the loss of his brother, or his father—not that he'd been in England for either death.

Just as he was giving up hope, the butler reappeared. "Please follow me, Lord Leighton."

He was led into a beautiful parlor, decorated in shades of blue. Lady Beatrix sat in an armchair by the window, although she stood when he entered. Even though she smiled in greeting, he could see the sadness behind her eyes.

It was a sadness that had lived behind his own for years now.

She curtseyed and then gestured for him to take a seat. "Lord Leighton. How kind of you to visit."

"I wanted to convey my condolences, Lady Beatrix," he said, gripping his top hat in his hands and trying not to lose himself in her devastated blue eyes. "I was shocked to hear about the passing of your father, so soon after I saw you both in Bath…"

Her breath hitched and she looked away, and he was sure she was trying to hide tears. He hadn't come here to upset her, but clearly reminding her of Bath was the wrong thing to do.

"I know what it feels like, to lose someone you look up to…someone you… I wish you did not have to suffer that pain." He wanted to reach out and take her hands, to offer her some comfort as she had done when he had fled the ballroom at the Assembly Rooms, but of course he could not. One of her staff could come in at any time, and what on earth would they think of such a display?

"Thank you," she whispered, and she turned back to give him a watery smile. "A lot of people have told me they are sorry, but it did not feel like any of them truly understood my pain."

"Perhaps they have not known such a close relationship," Spencer offered. "I was told several times that the price for such love is the pain of grief… I'm not sure it helped at the time, but now I can see that I was lucky to have such a close family, even if the pain of losing them nearly destroyed me."

He had not planned to open up to Lady Beatrix about his deepest emotions, but there was something about her that just made him want to be honest. She had seen the worst of him already; he doubted anything he could say now would worsen her opinion of him.

The tears she had been trying to hide finally filled her eyes, but she simply blinked them away and held his gaze. "I think you are right. I just hope I can feel that way, soon. I knew he was ill… Perhaps it should not have been such a shock. But it was. And I feel—"

She broke off, but he urged her to continue. "You feel?"

"I haven't told anyone this. But I cannot help but wonder if it was my fault. If persuading him to go to Bath hastened his end. I feel so guilty…"

"That will eat you up if you let it," Spencer said softly. "I do not believe your father would have gone if he had not thought it was for the best." Unless he thought there was no hope either way, Spencer thought to himself, but he did not voice that out loud. She did not need to add to her woes. "My brother died in front of me, on the battlefield. I have felt guilty every day since, for not saving him, for not being the one killed. But there is nothing you could have done to save your father—it was simply his time. And he got to spend his final days with the daughter he loved, in a beautiful city. You mustn't feel guilty, Lady Beatrix."

As his impassioned speech came to an end, he noticed her eyes were wide and wondered if he had said too much. It was that unique "something" about her, and the grief filling the room, that had loosened his tongue so.

She reached forward, and took his hand in hers, and his heart raced.

"It wasn't your fault, either," she said, her blue eyes looking at him so intently, he felt she could see straight into his soul. "Your brother chose his path, as we all do. It's a tragedy, but you cannot blame yourself. You didn't shoot him."

Her words shot straight to his heart, both painful and soothing, like ice-cold water, and he felt breathless. He did not know how long they sat like that, hearts aching and hands clasped, before the parlor door flew open, and they shot apart.

"Henderson said we had company," the tall gentleman,

whom Spencer had never seen before, announced.

He got to his feet and bowed. "Lord Leighton, at your service. I came to offer my condolences to Lady Beatrix."

The gentleman narrowed his eyes and did not look best pleased to see him.

"Lord Leighton," Lady Beatrix said, glancing between the two. "May I introduce Lord Haxbury. My father's heir."

They shook hands, and Spencer tried to read from her body language how Lady Beatrix felt about this man. Oddly, he could read his body language quite clearly, and it wasn't welcoming and was, in fact, a bit territorial. Of his new title and holdings or Lady Beatrix herself—of that, he couldn't be sure. Of course, Spencer knew she could not inherit her father's title, but he hadn't supposed the new heir would be found and brought to London quite so quickly.

BEATRIX KNEW SHE shouldn't have been holding Lord Leighton's hand. And yet, for the second time in a handful of weeks, there she was, doing so. Once again, she'd felt the need to comfort him, even though he had been comforting her.

And his words of comfort rang true. She didn't feel anyone else understood. Some clearly saw her grief as a display of far too much emotion. Others seemed surprised that she was so devastated when they clearly thought she ought to have known that Papa's end was near.

No one had spoken to her, soul to soul, like Lord Leighton had. He understood—because he felt so many of the same things.

And she could not help but take his hands and tell him that it was not his fault. Because, of course, it wasn't. His brother had gone to war—a terrible, dangerous path to follow—and the worst had happened. Lord Leighton couldn't have stopped it, and what good would it have been if he had been the one killed instead?

Then his brother would have felt the same guilt, surely.

But just as she'd been ready to tell him so, Lord Haxbury had come in. She didn't think he'd seen them holding hands, for that would surely create a terrible scandal—and he would be unlikely to still wish to wed her. Not that she had given him an answer yet. But she did not want the option taken away from her, no matter how distasteful she found it.

She had very few options open to her at all.

There was a tension between the two lords that she could not dispel. She did not think she would have been able to, even if she had been feeling entirely herself.

"I shan't disturb you. I merely wanted to inform you that the maids are moving my things into the master chamber, so if there are any personal effects of your father's you wish to remove, please do so."

The words stabbed her heart like a dagger. He had every right to the room, of course—but she had hoped he would wait until she left to take it. Unless she didn't leave… But the idea of sharing that room with him was too difficult to contemplate.

"Good day, Lord Leighton. A pleasure to meet you." And with that, he swept from the room, leaving Beatrix and Lord Leighton alone once more, although in a rather different atmosphere.

They took their seats again, and Beatrix didn't really know what to say. She was rather embarrassed at Lord Haxbury's rudeness, but she wasn't going to apologize for him. He was her family, but so distantly that she had barely known he existed before his arrival. If she married him… Well, then she would have to apologize. But she had not made that decision yet.

"So, your father's heir has arrived…"

Beatrix nodded. "Yes. He was on his way to London when he heard of his inheritance, and wished to make a start on the accounts."

Lord Leighton glanced towards the open door, as if to check that Lord Haxbury was not listening outside it, and then turned back to her with a frown.

"This cannot be easy for you…"

Beatrix gave a wry smile. "It is not. But there is nothing to be done. Things change when people die, and I'm in no position to argue it. Life doesn't always go the way you planned—and now I need to find the right path forward."

"Life certainly moves in strange ways. If it did not, I would not be a marquess, and I would not jump at every loud noise." His cheeks flushed, as though he had not meant to say that out loud, but she was glad he had—even if it could lead nowhere, she was glad to know more about this man who had dominated her dreams for years. Even if the knowledge was incredibly sad.

The clock struck noon, and Lord Leighton stood. "I should leave you in peace. But if there's ever anything you need, please know that I am a friend."

When he had left she called for fresh tea, and sat at the window, watching people passing by. The Season was coming to a close, and soon London would be much quieter. Normally she and Papa would have been thinking about returning to the country soon, but now everything was different. She had not found any promising positions in the magazines she had procured, and Lord Haxbury's proposal had a time limit on it.

She watched Lord Leighton walk away and tried to clear her mind of the fog of grief and see a path forwards. Lord Leighton had said he was her friend…and she was glad that he had come, even if their relationship was confusing and did not strictly follow society's rules.

He was her friend, and he clearly did not wish to be anything more. Her dreams of a life with him, which she had harbored since she was seventeen years old, needed to be put to one side.

He understood her so. And when they touched, she felt sparks shooting through her body. But she did not have time to wait for something to potentially grow, when he had said himself that he was broken.

She did not even think he wanted a wife.

And so her only options were to strike out on her own, or to wed the new Lord Haxbury.

And neither was very appealing.

CHAPTER SIXTEEN

"DID YOU RECEIVE an invitation to old Montgomery's house party next month?" Timothy asked as they enjoyed a glass of whisky at the club. "I think I'm going to attend, and then head back to Surrey. My betrothed is keen for the wedding plans to be finalized..."

"You have been putting it off," James said, and Spencer was pleased for the distraction. He had been invited to the house party, but could not bring himself to accept. He did not want to be scrutinized in a small, confined space where he would undoubtedly react to some loud noise and have everyone whispering about him. Or they would hear him having a nightmare, and think his brain was addled.

Timothy groaned. "You sound like Catherine. And my father..."

"I presume you want to marry the girl, since you asked her?"

"Well, yes, but asking and actually marrying are two very different things. I wanted to enjoy the Season first..."

"But the Season is almost over," James reminded him.

"Yes, yes, I know. So are you coming to the house party? My last hurrah before getting leg-shackled?" Timothy asked, raising his glass in the air and then downing the contents.

"Yes, I was thinking I would. It's on my way to the country, too—and Montgomery always has excellent fishing outings."

They both turned to look at Spencer, and he knocked back

the end of his drink. "I was invited, but I don't think I'll be attending. I still have business to take care of here…" The business the Marquess of Leighton really needed to attend to was back at the family seat in Wiltshire, where their land agent had been running things for far too long without any support or supervision.

But he couldn't bring himself to return yet.

"We don't want to leave you in London all summer…" Timothy said, his gaze flicking to James.

Irritation, however unfair it was, rose in Spencer's chest. He was not a child that needed to be watched.

"You're welcome to come to Bracknall Place, when I journey back there," James said, and the irritation was dampened. "My mother, father and sister will be in residence, but it's large enough that you wouldn't have to see them often. If you wanted somewhere in the countryside to go, that doesn't hold memories…"

"That is very kind. I haven't finalized my plans yet, but I will write to you. Please, do not concern yourselves with me—enjoy the fishing and summer in the countryside. And I await the invitation to your nuptials, Timothy."

He tried to pretend that everything was as it was before, even though he knew it never could be. He didn't want to wander aimlessly through his life, but he did not know how to live with the guilt and grief that hung over him. He had tried to take Lady Beatrix's words to heart, to believe that it was not his fault that Jack had died, that he had not profited from a death he could have stopped from occurring.

But without her calm voice and soft hands on his, it was hard to believe.

AT BREAKFAST THAT morning, Lord Haxbury had reminded her

that he needed an answer to his proposal that day—as though she had not known. As though the thought of making such a decision had not kept her awake every night.

And yet still she did not have an answer for him.

Although the day looked likely to turn wet, she decided to go for a walk, wanting to clear her head and make her decision.

"Where are we going, milady?" Jemima asked, hurrying to keep up with her fast pace. "I think it might rain soon…"

"I need to visit…a friend." She had not decided until she had stepped out onto the street, but she knew she needed to put her childish dreams from her mind if she was to marry Lord Haxbury. It wasn't really appropriate for her to call on Lord Leighton, but she would have her maid with her, and it wouldn't be happening again. She had to know that there was no hope before she accepted the life that was before her.

"If you could keep this visit to yourself, Jemima, I would appreciate it. I…probably shouldn't be going, but I must."

Jemima didn't hesitate. "Of course, milady. But if you're in some kind of trouble…"

"I'm just trying to work out what I'm going to do with my life. Now…now that I'm alone. And Lord Haxbury has presented me with one option, but I don't know if I wish to take it."

"He wants to marry you, doesn't he?"

Beatrix stopped in shock. She had not spoken of the proposal to anyone, and there had been no one in the room when the words were uttered. So how did her faithful maid know?

"I—"

She didn't know whether to deny it or to cry on Jemima's shoulder about the choice she had to make.

"The way he looks at you…I could tell he was considering it. And it's not right for you to be sharing a roof with him, with you both unwed."

"I know, Jemima," Beatrix whispered, beginning to walk down the street again. "But what can I do?"

"Do you want to marry him?"

Such a direct question—and one she had been asking herself repeatedly.

"I...would not choose him," she said, feeling terrible for saying out loud, but wanting to be honest with herself and the maid who had been with her since she was an infant. "But to be able to stay in my home, surrounded by memories, with you still by my side..." She sighed. "There's a lot I would do for that opportunity."

Jemima nodded. "There aren't many options in this world for women, whether you're titled or not. Just make sure that whatever decision you make, it's one you can live with."

Beatrix appreciated her advice. And that was what she was trying to do, by visiting Lord Leighton one last time. Put to rest any silly hopes and dreams and focus on her future—a future where she hoped she would be happy.

She doubted the burden of grief would ever truly leave her, but it would surely ease a little...and she did not wish to find herself stuck in a marriage she did not want when that time came.

CHAPTER SEVENTEEN

WHEN THE SERVANT fetched him from his study to tell him there was a lady who wished to speak to him, Spencer had no idea whom to expect.

He certainly did not expect to see Lady Beatrix standing nervously in the hallway, a middle-aged maid behind her.

"Lady Beatrix. What a pleasant surprise…"

She gave a small smile. "I know this is rather unorthodox, but I hoped I might speak to you for a few moments."

"Of course," Spencer hurried to say. "Perhaps your maid would like to go to the kitchen for some refreshment? Unless you prefer she remain present…" He mentally kicked himself. She surely would not wish to be alone with him, not after how close they had become the last two times they had been left un-chaperoned.

But she surprised him. "That would be wonderful, thank you."

"The parlor is just down here. And please have some tea brought, Henderson, once you have seen to Lady Beatrix's maid."

As they walked the short distance down the corridor, Spencer tried to think why she would be there. He had told her that he was her friend, and that he would be there for her should she ever need it. But what did she need from him?

And why did his heart have to race every time he merely clapped eyes on her?

He rushed to remove a book he had left carelessly open on the coffee table. "Please, take a seat." He ensured that the door remained open, and knew that one of his staff would be in soon with the tea, but nonetheless he felt a thrill being alone with her, even though he knew it was wrong.

"I know I should not have come here," Lady Beatrix began. "But you were so kind to call on me the other day and empathize with me…that I felt I needed to speak with you before I made a big decision."

Spencer's eyes widened. What big decision did she have to make, and why on earth did his opinion matter?

"You are most welcome here, even if it is a little unusual," he said with a smile.

"Thank you. I must confess I do not feel all that welcome in my own home currently."

Spencer frowned. He knew that feeling—although his own discomfort was from ghosts of memories, not from living people moving in when he was at his lowest. He could not imagine how difficult it must be for her.

"I have no brothers, no husband, no sons, no one to rely upon. My nearest male relative is the man who is now Lord Haxbury—a man I only met this week. And so, as I'm sure you know, I am left with very little to call my own."

"It is a terrible and unfair situation," Spencer said, trying to work out what on earth he could do to help her. "And if there's anything I can do… If you need money, perhaps, or…"

Lady Beatrix smiled. "We may not know each other well, but I think you know that I would not take money from you. No, I will earn my keep if I have to, as a paid companion, or a governess. I have been looking into options on both fronts."

Sadness overwhelmed Spencer. It was silly, really, for he kept deciding he would never see her again. And yet if she left to live in the country as a companion or a governess, then he truly never would.

It also seemed very unfair that she should have to leave everything behind when she was already battling such grief. He reached forward without even thinking, and took her hand in his.

"I hope you know I would happily give you the money, if you needed it. Or if you need help finding a position, or with organizing the travel there... Lady Beatrix, I cannot say everything I wish to say, because I am not the man I once was. I cannot offer the things that I would like. But I hope you know that I want you to be happy, above all else."

He had said too much. He had admitted the depth of his feelings, and that there was no way he could act on them. He didn't know if it was fair to tell her that, but the words came spilling out with no way of stopping them.

She held onto his hands tightly, not interrupting his speech, and when he met her beautiful blue eyes, they were teary and full of something that looked like hope.

He leaned closer still, drawn to her beautiful full lips like a flower to the sun, and even though he knew it contradicted everything he had just said, and even though he knew it was wrong, he pressed his lips to hers and felt an explosion detonate inside his chest.

Never before had a kiss made Spencer's blood burn through his veins. Never before had he ignored all the rules of propriety and kissed an unwed lady—a lady in mourning, no less—in the middle of the day.

What would have happened if the parlor door had not crashed open, Spencer could not say. He didn't think he would have deflowered this innocent woman, but desire for her burned more strongly within him than anything else. But the door did crash open, and they flew apart, his heart racing and his mind whirling. As he tried to get a read on his own emotions, he realized that his fear was not of the crashing of the door, or the reminder of the guns, but for Lady Beatrix, and not wanting her to be caught in such a position.

"So sorry, my lord. There's a draft, and the door just got away from me. There's a storm brewing outside..."

There was a storm brewing inside Spencer, but one he could not give voice to.

"Not a problem," Spencer said, avoiding eye contact with Lady Beatrix as the footman arranged the tea things in front of them. Had he seen anything? Spencer was fairly sure his staff were discreet, but it wasn't a risk he really wanted to take. It was too late to do anything about it now, though.

When the footman left, the door still wide open, Spencer dared to look at Lady Beatrix. She was as beautiful as ever, even clad in black which made her pale skin look even more ghostly. Her lips were swollen, her cheeks red, and he had never been more tempted to do something dishonorable than he was in that moment.

"I'm sorry." He tried to get hold of himself. There were many reasons he could not pursue Lady Beatrix—and he just had to remind himself of them. It wouldn't be fair to her, this beautiful woman, to be tied to a man who was afraid of his own shadow.

And then there was the fact that he did not think he could ever share a bedchamber with a woman while he was plagued so with nightmares. He struggled to know what was real and what was not in those dark hours, and the thought of someone else there beside him...

Well, normally it filled him with fear. But with Lady Beatrix before him, looking rather ravished, it was hard to focus on that.

"I... I quite understand," Lady Beatrix said with a blush, and he dared to hope—even though it would be a pointless hope— that she felt a similar desire for him as he did for her.

"If there's anything I can do to help though, as your friend... Please know that I will."

THE HOPE DIED in Beatrix's heart at those words.

He was a good man in many ways, and it was sweet that he

wanted to help her—but he clearly did not want anything more. Oh, she did not doubt that he desired her, and there was something thrilling about that. But if he had even considered marrying her, he surely would not be reminding her that he was her friend, not after kissing her like that.

She was grateful at least that she had experienced such a thrilling kiss before she was married. She had kissed Ambrose, but it had never ignited within her the feelings that Lord Leighton was capable of. The man set her body on fire with a single touch, and she did not even know his first name.

And now she doubted she ever would.

"Thank you for your friendship, my lord. The new Earl of Haxbury has asked for my hand in marriage, and I believe I shall accept. I thought, as we are friends, that you ought to know."

This was it. If he did not make an objection, then there was no hope left at all.

His eyes widened, and he picked up an empty cup, before realizing there was nothing in it and putting it back on the saucer. "I see. Well… I wish you every happiness."

So that was that. She would put aside her childish dreams, marry the new heir, and look forward to her life as a wife, mistress of the household, and hopefully one day, mother.

She fought back the tears that came to her eyes. She had done enough crying of late. And how could she feel like she was losing something, when she'd never had it to begin with?

"I won't take up any more of your time," she said before he had a chance to pour the tea. She could not bear to sit with him and make polite conversation when her heart was breaking. "Thank you, for your hospitality."

⇒⟩⟩⟩⟨⟨⟨⇐

HE RANG THE bell, and Henderson returned, before scurrying back downstairs to fetch Lady Beatrix's maid. He couldn't think straight. So many things had happened that he could never have imagined. And now she almost seemed angry, or cold at least, but he did not know what to say.

She was surely offended that he had kissed her. That would make sense. And she was right to be—he should not have done it. And yet…he could not bring himself to regret it.

If she was to wed another man, at least he knew what it felt like to kiss her. He doubted he would ever kiss another woman again who stirred such passion within him.

"Good day, Lord Leighton," she said with a bobbed curtsy as soon as her maid was present.

"Goodbye, Lady Beatrix."

For it had to be goodbye, he told himself as he returned to the parlor and poured himself a cup of very well-stewed tea. She had come here to tell him… Well, he presumed she had come here to tell him she was to be married. And he had kissed her. What a cad he was.

As he sipped his tea and wished it was late enough for something stronger, he tried to force away the thought that had been in his mind ever since she had left.

She's marrying him?

He knew it wasn't any of his business. She could marry whomever she chose—and he could certainly see the benefits of the match. She would not have to leave behind everything she had ever known.

And yet… Spencer had not liked the man when he'd met him. The way he'd come in so heavy-handed and announced he would be taking her father's room, without a moment's concern for her grief. And he was surely at least fifteen years her senior. A woman like that deserved someone who worshiped the ground she walked on.

He might have been that man, once upon a time. But he could not offer her what she needed, and so it was best that she married the new Lord Haxbury. She surely liked him, if she was going to marry him, so what did it matter if Spencer didn't care for him?

He would quite probably not see either of them again—and certainly not until the following Season, if he was even in London then.

She needed to find her path in the world, and he needed to find his.

CHAPTER EIGHTEEN

B EATRIX FELT AS though she might be sick as she knocked on the door to her father's—now the new Lord Haxbury's— study. She had promised him a decision within a week, and she had made it. Now she just needed to inform him.

He smiled at her when she entered, and she hoped that signaled the possibility of happiness in their future.

"Lord Haxbury. May I speak with you?"

"Of course. Take a seat. And I think, with us living so closely, you really ought to call me 'Thomas'."

The name stuck in her throat, but of course, he was right. They could not stand on ceremony forever.

"Thomas." She tried it out as she sat down. She ought to tell him to drop the 'Lady' from her own name, but she could not quite bring herself to. "I have thought long and hard about your proposal. And I do agree, it is the most sensible option for both of us."

His eyes lit up. "Marvelous. I knew you were a sensible girl. Now, I may be able to procure a special license, but—"

Beatrix bit her bottom lip. "I have one request. I really do not wish to wed until I am out of mourning." She gestured to her black dress—something she knew she would be expected to give up once she became a wife. No one wanted a wife who started their marriage mired in grief.

She knew the grief would not magically leave her when she

started wearing colors again. And yet it felt disrespectful to her father not to observe a proper mourning period.

Thomas leaned back in her father's—his—chair and furrowed his brow. "How long did you intend to remain in mourning for?" His tone made it clear her request was an inconvenience, but she did not intend to back down.

"I had thought six months," she said, but at the sound of Thomas's protests, she quickly added, "But I would be content with three."

"Well," Thomas said, loosening his cravat slightly. "Three months…could be feasible. It is not really appropriate though, for us to live here alone, unwed. Before it was unusual, but when we are betrothed, it will court scandal. And you understand that I have been very careful to choose a wife who will not bring scandal to my new title."

Beatrix nodded, more aware than ever that she had been selected for her breeding and her good behavior, and not her personality at all. "I had thought about that, my l—Thomas. I do have an aunt I could ask to stay, although she lives in the north and would take some time to arrive. And when she writes, it seems she is not well enough to travel very far. Perhaps we could hire a female companion, or…"

Thomas stroked his chin, although there was no hair there to be seen. "My sister does not live far from here. I have not seen her in several years…but she might be persuaded to stay with us, so that everything is above board."

Beatrix smiled. Perhaps his sister could be a friend in this strange new life she was living in. "An excellent plan. Then we agree on the betrothal, and a wedding in three months?"

"We do. I think we should have a glass of port to celebrate, don't you? And to toast the future Lord Haxbury, whose arrival we will all look forward to."

The thought made her feel rather sick, but there was no backing out now. She knew that an heir was what he wanted— and she did want children herself. It was just that, from the very little she knew about how a baby came to be, she did not like the idea of procreating with Thomas.

At least she would have three months to get used to the idea.

Thomas picked up his quill and returned to his documents the moment he had finished his glass of port, even though Beatrix's was still quite full. "I must send word to my sister immediately, and get the arrangements in order. I'm sure you understand…"

It was clearly a dismissal, and she stood with her glass of port and awkwardly left the room.

Back in the parlor, which had always been a room she had inhabited far more than her father, she sat in the window seat and sipped her port, which tasted more like a drink of commiseration than one of celebration. She had spent her life looking for magic, and she'd thought she'd found it that night in Vauxhall Gardens, on the precipice of adulthood. But she knew now that it was a childish fantasy. She would have to find the magic in life for herself, for she certainly was not going to get it from the heir to her father's title, or from daydreaming about a match that was not to be.

WITH MOST OF the ton having left for the countryside, the club was quiet. Spencer wasn't really sure why he'd come. He didn't want to see anyone particularly, and he knew his friends had already left for the house party. But he could not bear to sit at home with his own thoughts any longer.

Since Lady Beatrix's visit, and that kiss, he'd found it hard to get her from his mind. His preoccupation with her in the day seemed to lead to worse nightmares once he retired to bed, although he did not understand the connection. All he knew was that he awoke two or three times a night screaming and thrashing, trapped in his sheets, begging for his brother's life.

Seeing his brother die once had been hard enough. But reliving it every night, sometimes more than once, in his dreams was harrowing. If only there was some remedy…but the nightmares were getting worse instead of better.

And so he did not sleep well at night, and during the day he spent time alone in his study, trying to focus on paperwork but instead finding his mind wandering to Lady Beatrix.

Why had she come to his home that day? Was it truly just to inform him she was to be betrothed? She'd had no obligation to do so, since there was nothing officially between them. If she felt the spark that he did…well, she had not let on.

And that was probably for the best, since he could not, would not, ask her to be his wife.

But he had kissed her…and she had not pulled away, or berated him. That kiss would be seared onto his soul until the day he died.

He was on his second whisky when a group of gentlemen, none of whom he recognized thanks to his reclusive ways, settled at the table beside him. Their chatter was rather ribald, and he did not listen closely to what they were saying until he heard a name he recognized.

"I bet he couldn't believe his luck," a fair-haired man said, a slight slur to his words. "From what I heard, he didn't have much to his name. A few gambling debts, a small house in the middle of nowhere, never even met his titled family… And all of a sudden he's an earl! Just like that."

"Was Haxbury old? I didn't know him," a dark-haired gentleman asked.

"He wasn't young…but he wasn't ancient. In poor health for a while though, I heard."

"What a shame not to have a son to inherit, or a younger brother or someone more closely related. No offense to the new Lord Haxbury, but I shouldn't like to think of my title and everything I've worked for going to someone I'd never met."

Although it was the name of Haxbury that had pricked Spencer's ears, the sentiment struck him harder than he would have expected. Would Jack have been pleased to know that the title had been passed to his younger brother, when he himself should have inherited it? And how would he feel about Spencer's inability to marry, knowing that he would never have children to inherit the title, but would instead pass it on to some unknown cousin after his own death? Just like Lord Haxbury...

"No, only a daughter. And did you hear? She's to marry the new earl—once she's out of mourning."

One of the gentlemen—Spencer didn't want to look over obviously to see which—let out a low whistle. "Well that's nice and neat, isn't it? She inherits nothing, but marries the heir. Makes sense."

"Yeah, it does. But how old is the new Lord Haxbury, do we know?"

"Approaching forty, I heard. And Haxbury's daughter must only be five-and-twenty, although she's never wed."

Spencer leaned a little closer as the conversation turned to Lady Beatrix.

"The daughter of an earl, unwed? Does she have some deformity? Or some terrible character flaw?" the fairer gentleman asked.

Spencer clenched his fists under the table, feeling angry at the way they were discussing her. Although he himself could not understand why she hadn't been married to someone younger and far more eligible many years earlier.

Some part of him had been pleased when they'd met again in Vauxhall Gardens that she didn't have a husband, and yet now he regretted that selfish thought. If she had been married when her father had died, she wouldn't have had to make a quick choice about her future.

Maybe then she wouldn't be marrying the new Lord Haxbury—whom Spencer found he did not like.

And yet she deserved to have a marriage to someone who could look after her, give her children, someone whole and healthy without ghosts haunting him.

"No, she's quite pretty I believe. But she was involved with Trentham—do you remember him?"

"The notorious rake? Killed in a duel?"

"That's the one."

"Well, that'll certainly damage marriage prospects."

"She was betrothed to him when he died, from what I remember. So he was going to do the right thing—well, until he got involved drunkenly in that duel."

Spencer stood abruptly, his chair scraping the wooden floor, and stalked from the room. He'd heard enough. He did not wish to hear those men gossiping about Lady Beatrix, and nor did he believe what they were saying. It was better to leave before his anger caused him to make a scene. He struggled to control his emotions these days. One moment he was spooked by a loud bang; the next he felt furious at the words of a friend, or a stranger.

And he didn't want to make a scene. What was the point? Lady Beatrix was marrying Lord Haxbury. She would have children with him, and the title of Haxbury would pass to her sons, and everything would continue as it ought to.

CHAPTER NINETEEN

HE DID NOT truly know what changed his mind. He did not think it was loneliness, for it was easier to hide his despair and pitiful actions when he was alone. And yet when he was alone, there was too much time to think…

To think on the war. To think on his losses. To think on Lady Beatrix, and the man she would marry.

The man who was not, and could not, be him.

As much as he might wish it.

He rode hard and fast to try to wipe out the images in his mind of Lady Beatrix…images of her as his wife.

And even more troubling ones of her as Haxbury's wife.

He had chosen to ride, rather than take a carriage, to Montgomery's house party. It was rather foolish, since it was two days' ride and the weather in England was hardly predictable, but sitting in a carriage gave too much time for thinking.

And besides, Spencer was in great shape. A by-product of those years on French battlefields was a strong, muscled physique, and so much nervous energy that he did not think he would ever be in danger of running to fat. A two-day ride was no hardship for him at all. And even when the heavens opened, leaving him soaked through by the time he arrived at the inn he had chosen for the night, he could not bring himself to be sorry he had traveled on horseback.

There were many things in his life he was sorry for. And he

thought he might well regret attending this house party, where he would not so easily be able to hide from the world.

But at least he would not do anything foolish, like visiting Lady Beatrix, or kissing her, or begging her to marry him.

All three actions would surely be ruinous—for them both.

Montgomery would surely think him very eccentric, turning up to a house party two days late, on horseback, having declined the invitation and without a valet. But he was sure his old university colleague would still open his doors to him, and undoubtedly provide him with a valet to ensure he was presentable for the party. And although he had no desire to make conversation or gamble or flirt with pretty ladies, his friends were right—there was always good fishing to be had at Monty's. And that would surely take his mind off his troubles.

It was nearly noon when he arrived at the grand country home of the Viscount of Dalkeith. He was hungry, dusty, and tired as he jumped from his horse. He grabbed his smarter clothes from the saddlebag and thanked the stable boy who appeared swiftly to lead his mount away.

"She's been worked hard, so make sure she's well-fed," he said. The boy nodded and grinned at the silver coin Spencer tossed his way.

"Yes milord. Of course."

Spencer caught sight of himself in a lower window and almost laughed. He might be turned away, for fear he was a vagrant. The dust of the road covered him, and his black hair looked dull and in need of a comb. But it was nothing a good bath and a change of clothes could not fix. If only all his problems were so easily solved.

When the butler opened the door, Spencer introduced himself immediately to avoid any misunderstandings. "The Marquess of Leighton, here to see the Viscount," he said with a smile. "He may not be expecting me, but I was invited…"

The short butler bowed his head and took a step back. "Of course, my lord. Please come in. His lordship and his guests are currently out on a picnic, but if you would like to wait in the parlor…"

It was lucky for the house party guests that the rain of the previous day seemed to be staying away, although the clouds were not entirely friendly.

"Thank you. Perhaps I could change and freshen up, before they arrive? It was a hard ride."

"Of course, my lord. I will show you to a chamber, and have hot water brought up. And perhaps something to eat, since you have missed the picnic?"

Spencer grinned. "It's like you can read my mind."

He felt energized by the hard ride and the distance between himself and London, and the person on his mind. Perhaps he ought to have got away to the country sooner, he thought to himself as he stripped off his dirty clothes and washed his face and hair as best his could with the basin of warm water. Later that night he would ask for a bath, he decided—presuming his host did not ask him to leave, since he had technically declined the invitation.

As he redressed and wolfed down the sandwiches that had been sent up, he wondered if he would feel so invigorated if he went to his own country seat of Sythmore Abbey in Wiltshire. He did not think so. He had avoided it for a reason. There were far too many memories there. But perhaps he could escape else-where, once the house party was through. James had offered for him to accompany him to his family home, Bracknall Place. Or he could choose another of the homes he now owned. Hell, he could purchase a new property. He was not without wealth, now that he was the marquess—and he had no idea what to do with it all. He was not a gambler, and he had no son to build an inheritance for. He did not expect to ever have a wife or children to provide for—so why not spend some of the money he had never really wanted on a place to escape to from the city? Somewhere with no memories to haunt him at all.

The sound of hooves and chattering voices broke his reverie, and he moved to the window to see the house party returning. He recognized Montgomery, and Timothy and James of course, but the rest of the guests—one other male and three females—were unknown to him. He took a deep breath and checked his appearance in the mirror. A wash and a change of clothes had done him a world of good. He looked the part of a marquess now—however little he felt like one.

When he made his way downstairs, he found they were waiting for him in the parlor. The butler had obviously announced his arrival, because no one looked shocked.

"This is a pleasant surprise, Spencer," Montgomery said, clapping him on the back with a cheerful grin. The red head had always been of a cheery disposition, and Spencer could not help but smile back.

"I hope you'll forgive me for changing my mind after I had sent my regrets."

"Of course! The more the merrier. And we've plans to fish tomorrow, so you've not missed that. Now, you know James and Timothy, of course. And this is Mr. Templeton, from Hounslow."

A tall, dark-haired gentleman with a serious face reached out his hand to shake Spencer's. "Pleased to make your acquaintance, Lord Leighton."

"And we're honored with the presence of these three lovely young ladies—Lady Daphne Harrow, and Misses Jennifer and Louisa Trentbridge. Ladies, allow me to present the Marquess of Leighton."

The three ladies curtseyed and smiled, and one of the misses Trentbridge—Spencer thought she was Louisa—batted her eyelashes at him. The ladies were clearly eyeing up this new guest as potential marriage material—which he most certainly was not.

Spencer smiled politely, and quickly made his way to Timothy and James, who expressed how unexpected his arrival had been.

"London get boring without us?" Timothy asked.

He laughed at his friend's arrogance. "Something like that."

"Well, it's good to see you here. And Monty has promised a marvelous day tomorrow, too—it's nice to get out of the city and be able to really ride, isn't it!"

Spencer nodded. "It's certainly a good distraction."

CHAPTER TWENTY

THE LETTER FROM Aunt Elspeth was not entirely unsurprising. She had been too frail, she had said in her last letter, to return to see her niece after Papa had died, and Beatrix had for a while thought her austere aunt had washed her hands of her.

She had briefly considered visiting, when she had not known where to turn—but she had not wanted her aunt to quickly marry her off to whomever was most convenient.

Had her aunt heard of her betrothal? The question filled her mind as she opened the seal and sat in the window seat to read what her aunt had to say.

Beatrix,

I would like to see you in order to discuss your future. I am not strong enough to travel, and request that you attend me here at your earliest convenience.

Aunt Elspeth.

She reread the brief note more than once, trying to discern more meaning. Did her aunt think she had no plan in life? Or had she heard of the betrothal and disapproved? Or the contrary—did she wish to ensure the marriage went ahead?

She could of course have refused the invitation—although to call it such was a stretch of politeness, indeed it was more of a summons—since her aunt had no jurisdiction over her. But as her only living close relative, Beatrix hoped she had her best interests at heart—and she really was not sure if she had made the right decision about her future.

Perhaps her aunt would have some words of wisdom that would help her see what she ought to do, or to make the decision she had made more palatable.

It could hardly be less so.

She knocked on the study door, knowing Thomas would surely be in there with his ledger and a large glass of whisky. She did not know why she felt nervous; she was not yet his wife, and so she did not really need his permission. And besides, she was a grown woman, not some child.

"Ah, my dear," he said when she entered. The term of endearment made her skin crawl. "I have good news—my sister Sarah should be here in ten days or so."

Beatrix forced a smile. "Excellent. I have had news myself—my aunt has asked me to visit her. It is quite a ride, but I do feel I ought to share our news in person, and see that she is well cared for…"

Thomas frowned. "How long would you be away?"

"A week, I should think."

"If my sister arrives and you are not here…"

"I am sure I will return in time. The roads are good, and I shall only take Jemima, so there will be no inconvenience to you." She refused to ask his permission. She was of age, and as yet a free woman. A penniless one, perhaps, but a free woman all the same.

Until she wed him. Then she would be his, to bid as he pleased. The thought sent an uncomfortable chill down her spine.

"Very well," he said. "But make sure you only stay in respectable inns on the road. I do not wish my betrothed to have scurrilous rumors spread about her."

Beatrix nodded her head. "Of course," she agreed, and retreated from the room before her irritation showed. She had been raised as the daughter of an earl—did he really think she would so easily throw away her reputation? And he did not seem to have a care for her safety, should she choose disreputable inns to frequent…just her reputation. And therefore his.

The man really was an infuriating bore.

Still, she would take a week away from him, and when she returned, she hoped she would be able to accept her situation with more grace. After all, it was the only—and the best—option she had.

⟫⟪

THE JOURNEY TO Aunt Elspeth's was one she had always found long and arduous. Although she had been happy to spend the time with her papa, she had always felt very judged when they arrived in the north, with her aunt ready to criticize at every opportunity. And spending two days in a coach, when there were so many more interesting things she could be pursuing, had always frustrated her.

And yet now the hours in the coach felt like an escape. Alone with her maid Jemima, her sewing and a novel, she felt more at peace than she had done since before her dear papa had passed away.

Her heart ached for the loss of him, and yet she had more pressing concerns that she could not ignore: the cage she was about to lock herself in.

Marrying Thomas seemed like her only option, and yet she could not approach it with any joy. This trip to see Aunt Elspeth would at least get her away for a few days, with time to think and breathe. Perhaps her aunt would have a solution she had not thought of, and she would not have to marry a man she did not know, a man whose bed she did not wish share, a man who she did not think she could rely on.

If only the man she did wish to be her husband had suggested marriage. But alas, it was clear he only saw her as his friend, someone he would help if he could, but not a future wife.

She could not pin her hopes on a dream. She was too old and too alone in the world for that. Gone were the ideals of her eighteen-year-old self, who thought she would marry for love and enter a union as blissful as that of her parents.

That wasn't real life—she knew that now.

But perhaps there was an option other than the new Earl of Haxbury. She could only hope.

"We should stop before it gets dark, milady," Jemima said, glancing out of the carriage window at the setting sun. The day had quite disappeared, with Beatrix lost in thoughts, and she smiled at her long-time maid.

"Yes, of course. There's an inn not far ahead." They travelled with a coach driver and footman, who Thomas had begrudgingly agreed ought to accompany them for safety, and Beatrix did not think being stopped by highwaymen was likely, but Jemima was right—it was far safer to be off the roads by nightfall.

As they stopped outside the inn, she could not help a fanciful notion entering her head. What if she was taken by a highwayman, and thrown into a whole new life—one where she did not need to marry a man she did not wish to in order to secure her life.

Romantic dreams are not a reality, she reminded herself as she alighted from the carriage. When she was younger, she would have lost herself in such daydreams, but she no longer had that luxury.

Life as a penniless, unwed woman would not be some romantic dream. It would be an entirely different life to the one she had lived up until now. She had no skills to fall back on, no education past what was required to be a young lady in society. She might be able to find a position as a paid companion, or as a governess, if her knowledge could pass muster—but little beyond that.

And if she could not find a way to put a roof over her head, she had no one to turn to. She would never have her own home, her own children, her own life. And marrying Thomas offered that. Her childhood home as her own once more. She would be the lady of the house, and she would have children to raise and love, and the life that she had expected.

That was not such a bad outcome, was it?

***

DINNER WAS A loud and long affair, and Spencer found he was very out of practice with socializing. He had been placed between the lady who had batted her eyelashes—who he confirmed was Miss Louisa Trentbridge—and James, and he regularly had to remind himself not to only converse with his friend.

"I do not recall seeing you in London this season, Lord Leighton," she said with a smile when he turned to speak with her. "And I cannot imagine I would have missed you."

He forced a smile. "I was in London, but I do not frequent many balls I'm afraid."

"Oh that is a shame. Do you not like to dance?"

A memory of dancing with Lady Beatrix came to mind and he pushed it away. It was painful to think on such a perfect time, now that it was lost to him forever.

"Not particularly," he answered, not wishing to discuss why he did not enjoy society. "But I trust you enjoyed the Season?"

Miss Trentbridge nodded and smiled over at her sister on the other side of the table. "Oh yes. It was my first Season out, and my sister's second, and we enjoyed it more so for being together."

"A sibling relationship is a wonderful thing," he agreed, his heart aching at the words.

He and Jack had not enjoyed balls, but they had hunted together, drank together, played cards together.

Fought together.

"And then Mama was delighted that we were invited here, to

continue the fun of the season. Lord Dalkeith has been most generous in his hospitality."

Spencer glanced over at Montgomery, and saw the way he was smiling over at Miss Jennifer Trentbridge, and was sure he knew why the two sisters had been invited. He wondered if there would be a betrothal before the week was out. Far stranger things had happened at house parties, after all.

The ladies and gentlemen separated after dinner, but the separation did not last long, with the ladies claiming it was unfair to only have the three of them while there were five gentleman next door. The other four men laughed and smiled and seemed very happy with the arrangement, but Spencer was sure Miss Louisa would make a beeline for him, and he had no wish to flirt, or give false hope.

If he was not fit to marry the only woman he had ever seriously considered, he certainly wasn't going to marry any other.

"It's good to see you here, Spencer," James said, sipping his whisky beside him. "I'm glad you didn't stay in London."

Spencer nodded. "I think I am, too," he said with a slight smile. The countryside was certainly quieter, which helped his nerves—although the peace also risked him having more time to think.

"Did something happen, to change your mind?"

Spencer paused and drank his own drink for a minute. Had it? Certainly no big event. He had not done something stupid like declare his feelings for Lady Beatrix, or called out the fools in the club for their callous talk over her.

"Just the realization, I suppose, that I need to decide on a path. I cannot wallow in London forever."

James was saved the need for an answer by the rather expected arrival of Miss Louisa, with a pretty smile on her face and a glass of port in her hand.

"May I join you, gentlemen?" she asked, taking a seat before they had chance to reply. "My sister is trying to make up numbers for whist, and I am rather terrible at the game."

"Of course," James said, turning to include her in the conversation. "I have no love of whist myself."

"And you, Lord Leighton?" Miss Louisa asked. "Are you fond of card games?"

"Not particularly," Spencer answered honestly. "I do not like to gamble, and I prefer outdoor pursuits."

Miss Louisa beamed: "Something else we have in common!"

Spencer inwardly groaned. That had not been his intention. The girl was clearly hunting for a husband, and he had no wish to give her false hope.

"You are fond of music though, are you not?" James said. "Do you play the piano, Miss Trentbridge?"

She beamed and fluttered her eyelashes. "Oh yes, I love to play. Perhaps I could play something now, since no one is at the instrument."

As soon as she'd left, Spencer groaned. "Why are you encouraging the chit?" he asked his friend. "I do not wish her to think we have anything in common."

James laughed, carefree as always. "It's a house party, Spencer, romance is always on the cards. And besides, a little flirtation won't do you any harm!"

Spencer gritted his teeth. He had no interest in flirting, and certainly not with Miss Louisa Trentbridge. He had come away to distance himself from Beatrix, it was true—but not by searching for another woman to replace her in his mind.

Or in his heart.

He did not think that would ever happen—as ridiculous as that was, since she was really nothing to him, and he was even less to her. A footnote on her life. A memory of a dance; a single kiss before she married.

In five years' time, would she even remember his name?

"Well you are free to choose your own flirtations," Spencer snapped, more harshly than was warranted. "But please refrain from encouraging any on my behalf."

Miss Trentbridge began to play, and the company listened

politely. She was fairly accomplished, but while Spencer did indeed enjoy music, he didn't feel anything while she played.

Perhaps the war had washed away any ability he had for emotions.

Or perhaps he had just lost his heart…

CHAPTER TWENTY-ONE

S PENCER WAS PLEASED that their fishing expedition would take up most of the following day, for it meant spending time away from the ladies. He did not dislike them, but he did not wish to be rude—and he thought he would have to be discourteous in order to make it clear to Miss Trentbridge that he would not be courting her.

The day dawned fine and bright, and he was relieved to see no dark clouds in the sky. A hard ride across the estate and a day on the lake was just what he needed to get his mind off London, off Lady Beatrix, and off what he was going to do next. Before the war, he had enjoyed hunting, but he still could not bear to hold a gun in his hand, let alone hear the shots ringing out around him.

He wondered if Montgomery had chosen fishing for that reason, or whether it was simply fortuitous.

Even without his unfortunate reaction to gunshots, he didn't think he would have the stomach for hunting any more. Especially when it came to hunting for pleasure, when the quarry wasn't even consumed. His feelings towards shooting and killing for fun had changed drastically since before the war.

"Your grounds are idyllic, Montgomery," James said as they rode over to the lake on the far side of the estate.

"It makes me think I really must oversee some improvements to the grounds at Linton House… Father is quite happy for me to live there, but since I'm so often in the city, I confess I have not really put much thought into maintaining the place," Timothy said, riding up alongside them. "But when I'm here… I can see the value of a good groundsman and making sure things are kept on top of."

"Your wife may wish to have a say in where you live and how things are done," James said, a cheeky smile on his face. They all knew that Timothy's future wife—whenever he got around to wedding her—was not his favorite topic of conversation.

"Oh yes, I always forget that you're betrothed. Has a date been set?" Montgomery asked.

Timothy sighed and shook his head. "After this house party, when I return home, I suppose it shall become necessary to do so. My father—and the lady in question—are unlikely to brook further delays."

Montgomery chuckled. "Been enjoying your freedom, have you?"

"Just as all of you have," Timothy said hotly. "I don't hear wedding bells for any of you."

James just laughed. "You asked the girl to marry you, Timothy. I'm not sure I feel much sympathy. Besides, you never know what might happen at a house party. Perhaps a church is in someone else's future here…"

Spencer wasn't sure if this was a joke at his expense about Miss Trentbridge's interest in him, but he soon realized from the looks toward Montgomery that it was his flirtation with the elder Miss Trentbridge they were referring to.

Montgomery simply smiled. "Who's to say? But I certainly don't view marriage as the shackle you do, Timothy. I understand the girl may have been of your parents' choosing, but are you so sure that marriage will be a terrible decision?"

Timothy looked uncomfortable. Up until now, none of them had pressured him about his reluctance to marry—though, privately, Spencer thought it rather unfair that Timothy had agreed to marry the girl and still had not set a date.

"I don't like feeling like my life is decided for me," he said with a pout that was erring on the childish.

"No one likes to feel that," James said more kindly as they approached the lake. "But if you really don't wish to wed her, then perhaps you should say something now, rather than just letting things drag on."

Spencer stayed quiet as they dismounted and set up their rods. He did not wish to comment on anyone's romantic interests—and even less did he wish to discuss his own.

Apparently, though, that would not be so easy to avoid.

They had been fishing for about an hour, with only a couple of bites between them, when Montgomery turned his attention to Spencer. "No marriage on your horizon, then, Leighton?" he asked. As usual, Spencer bristled a little at the sound of his title.

"No," he said simply, and rather too brusquely.

But that did not deter Montgomery. "I know you did not expect to inherit, but you are a marquess now—surely you have some thoughts on who will inherit the title?"

Spencer's hands tightened around the rod, and he had to be careful not to snap it. Why could they not understand? The title wasn't supposed to be his. He was not the one who was meant to be thinking about the next Marquess of Leighton. He was too broken to think of a wife, to think of the future at all. Even being here was a step he would not have taken six months previously.

He did not wish to be rude, but frustration filled his words anyway. "I have no interest in who inherits after me."

After all, he would be dead and gone, so why did it matter?

Montgomery seemed silenced by his rudeness, but James and Timothy were not. Perhaps they were just used to it; perhaps they thought there was something to gain from pushing him.

"We thought, perhaps, you might offer for Lady Beatrix..." James said nonchalantly.

At the mention of her name, Spencer's hands tightened even more, and the rod began to bend.

"Lady Beatrix who?" Montgomery asked, intrigued.

"Chichester," Timothy supplied helpfully. "The old Earl of

Haxbury's daughter."

"Oh yes, I know who you mean. I heard she's quite pretty, although never wed for some reason. She'd be a suitable marchioness, would she not, Spencer?"

"There will not be another Marchioness of Leighton," Spencer snapped, loud enough to scare the fish away and make his companions look up in surprise.

"I'm sorry," he said through gritted teeth. "But can we please drop the subject. Now."

⟫⟫⟫✦⟪⟪⟪

BY THE TIME they reached Aunt Elspeth's home, Beatrix was keen to see her aunt. It was not an emotion she had felt before, but her aunt *was* her last close relative, and she wanted to feel like she belonged somewhere.

Unfortunately, her enthusiasm in the meeting was not reciprocated.

The hallway was empty and drafty when the butler showed her and Jemima in, and there was no fire lit in the parlor. It did not feel very welcoming at all, and Beatrix felt rather disappointed—until the butler explained that her aunt preferred to keep to her rooms these days.

Perhaps she is more sick than I thought. Perhaps age has hit her like it did dear Papa, she thought, feeling guilty.

"I will go to her," she said, removing her traveling cloak. "If you could show my maid to my room, I will go straight to Aunt Elspeth's," she said, taking the stairs two at a time.

She knocked on the door before entering, and the sight that greeted her was, thankfully, not of her aunt in bed, but sitting by the fireplace, a tea tray before her.

"Good afternoon, Aunt Elspeth," Beatrix said, warmth in her voice. "I hope you are well."

Her aunt turned her head and focused her piercing eyes upon her. "So you came at last. Good, come and sit down—although you could have fixed your hair before coming to see me."

Beatrix faltered in her step. Somehow she had forgotten just how critical her aunt could be. She smoothed the escaped locks back into her chignon and forced a smile on her face. "My apologies, aunt. I have been traveling for some time, and was concerned when we arrived that you might be sick."

Her aunt tutted. "I may be getting old, but I'm not so ancient that I don't know how a young lady should behave. Now, I can see you're still in full mourning. I applaud the sentiment—you know I had a fondness for my brother. But you must not let it stand in your way."

Beatrix took a seat opposite her aunt, and wondered how rude it would be to suggest ringing for some more tea. She was desperate for a drink herself.

"I don't understand, why would it stand in my way?" Beatrix asked with a frown.

Aunt Elspeth tutted loudly. "You must wed, girl. Surely you know that. You should have married before your father died—and perhaps, without that ridiculous Trentham affair, you would have done. But that's by the by—you have no money, no dowry, and you are fast approaching being an old maid. You're not unattractive, but looks fade—and you need a husband sooner rather than later."

Beatrix winced at her aunt's cruel appraisal of her situation in life. Of course, she knew she needed to wed. And it upset her that she had been out so many Seasons without finding a suitable match that she wished to pursue... Well, other than one man. But there was no use thinking about him.

"I have in fact received a proposal of marriage," she said, without thinking. She wasn't even sure she wanted her aunt's opinion on the union with Thomas—but it was hard to hear her character take such a bashing without retorting.

Aunt Elspeth's eyebrows disappeared into her hairline. "You have?"

Beatrix stuck out her chin. There was no turning back now.

"Yes. But I have asked that we wait to wed until I am out of mourning."

Aunt Elspeth shook her head. "Foolish girl. You don't have time on your side. Who is this man, anyway? Does he have a good name? Money? An estate?"

The barked questions made Beatrix sad. Of course her aunt didn't care whether the man was good or kind or had stolen Beatrix's heart. He just needed to be wealthy.

Which, of course, he was.

"His name is Thomas. And he is the new Earl of Haxbury."

"My, you work quickly. I am surprised, with how you have conducted yourself these past few years. But that sounds like a fine match... You will make a respectable countess. You will be provided for. You will pass your father's title onto your own son one day. Yes, very neat." She almost looked proud of her, and Beatrix might have felt some warmth from that, except she had done nothing to deserve the praise—and her heart very much sank at the thought of her very neat, very suitable match.

"What if..." Beatrix began, fiddling with a loose thread on her black skirt. "What if he is not the right choice?"

Aunt Elspeth's frown returned. "The right choice? My dear girl, you are five-and-twenty, with no father, no brother, no money, no estate. What choices do you think you have?"

Beatrix sighed. "I do know that, Aunt, I really do," she said, and it was true—her aunt was only telling her the reasons she herself had come up with to say yes to Thomas. "But I do not wish to spend my life unhappy..."

"Unhappiness is a choice," Aunt Elspeth barked. "You may have had the luxury of choosing a man you were confident you would be happy with at seventeen—although if my brother had any sense, he would have arranged a good match for you that first Season—but now you most definitely do not. Accept the match and be grateful for it. What will you do otherwise? Live on the streets?"

Her harsh laugh turned into a cough, and Beatrix blinked

away tears. "I could be a governess, or a companion, or—"

"You were born the daughter of an earl. You should be married and giving birth to a great line. If you decline this match, there will be no support for you here, believe that. You have turned down many matches, and then there was that foolish business with Trentham. You need to stop daydreaming girl, and make the right choice."

"Yes Aunt Elspeth," Beatrix said miserably, struggling to accept that Thomas really was the right choice.

CHAPTER TWENTY-TWO

IN SPITE OF the fractious conversation, the fishing trip was a
success. They all caught plenty, some of which would be sent
down to the village to feed the poor, and some of which would
grace their dinner table. Women had not been mentioned again,
and that led to a much more convivial atmosphere on the ride
home.

There was just time when they returned to the house for a
hot bath and a change of clothes before dinner. The busy
schedule of the house party kept time moving quickly, and
Spencer allowed himself a few moments to soak in the copper tub
and let his mind wander.

Beatrix.

Her name being mentioned today had surprised him. As had
his reaction to the thought of her. He had been avoiding letting
her into his mind, because she was so hard to get out again. But
now, just for a moment, enveloped by the warm water and the
smell of the lavender soap, he allowed himself to think of her.

To imagine things were different.

If he had not followed his brother onto the battlefield—in
fact, if his brother had not gone at all. He would have remained
Lord Clement, second son. And if his father had still passed away
at the same time, he would have then become younger brother to
the marquess.

He would have called on Lady Beatrix, once she was out in

society. He would have called on her, and taken tea with her and her father, and asked to escort her round the park. All the things he and his friends had thought silly and foppish back then—but he would have done them, for her.

They would have danced at balls, and he would have courted her and asked her father for her hand. He was sure of it. There had been something between them that night at Vauxhall Gardens. Something that in his youth he would have laughed off, but that now he could appreciate. And the spark was still there, even though the years had taken their toll on them both.

And yet now it was too late. He was too broken to be a good husband, and she was betrothed to another man. His days of romance were long past—and yet, for a few minutes in the rapidly cooling bath, he allowed himself to imagine what it would be like if things had gone to plan.

Perhaps they would be at this house party still—but together.

Perhaps they would happily be ensconced in the countryside, ignoring the world and enjoying their own little bubble of happiness.

Perhaps they would have a brood of children, none of whom were ever likely to be marquess, but all of whom would be loved desperately.

He sank under the water to wash the dreams away. Dreams were just as painful as nightmares, in a way. When all was said and done, you still had to come back to reality—and his reality was an evening of socializing without the woman of his dreams by his side.

By the time Spencer retired for the night, he was exhausted. The day's riding, fishing, and socializing had worn him out, and he was hopeful for a long, dreamless slumber. Not that he held out much hope for the dreamless part. Nightmares always came, whether he was happy or sad, tired or full of energy.

He didn't always remember the details, but he always recalled the fear, the panic, the twisted sheets, and the echo of his own screams. It was a penance he had resigned himself to paying for the rest of his life. The punishment for surviving the war, when his brother had not.

His attempts to cure himself with the waters at Bath had been foolish and unsurprisingly unsuccessful. Sometimes, he thought he deserved to feel so broken. After all, he had everything Jack should have had: the title, the future, the property. A life.

It wouldn't be fair if he was happy and at peace, too.

It was with such heavy thoughts that he closed his bedchamber door behind him with a sigh and loosened his cravat. When he turned, he let out an expletive that certainly should not have been uttered in front of a lady, and took a step backward.

Had he inadvertently entered the wrong chamber? That was his first assumption—but then he noticed his jacket on the armoire door and his comb on the dressing table, and he knew he had not.

Had she wandered into the wrong room? She had come to bed sometime earlier and was dressed in a sheer night rail that he certainly should not be seeing her in.

"Miss Louisa," he began, unsure where to look. She was an attractive woman, there was no denying that—but she was not his.

She would never be his.

He did not want her to be his…

There was only one woman he wanted dressed like that in his chamber—and she would also never be his.

"Lord Leighton," she said, her voice wavering a little as she spoke. "I thought, perhaps, we could spend some more time together. After all, the house party will soon end, and I had hoped we could become better acquainted…"

"This is not appropriate, madam," he said, his palms beginning to sweat. He didn't like to sound like some old man, but surely she knew what would happen if she was discovered here, in this state of undress?

She'd be ruined. They would have to wed. And she would be

tied to a broken man for the rest of her days—and he to a woman he could never love.

It didn't bear thinking about.

"We've been getting along, have we not?" she said, shyly looking to the floor and biting her bottom lip. Her attempted seduction was not having the desired effect. Was she trying to trap him into marriage? He'd been polite to her, certainly, but was sure he'd done nothing to make her think that a marriage proposal was likely.

"Miss Trentbridge, please leave and return to your chamber, before someone should discover you here."

"I thought we could speak more privately, just for a little while…"

Spencer was becoming frustrated. She was surely not as naive as she was trying to appear. This action seemed planned—and he would not be trapped into a marriage. Nor would he tie her to a broken man for the rest of her life. She did not know the man she was trying to net.

"I do not wish to be rude. But you have made a mistake, Miss Louisa. This is not something I desire, and you will regret it too. Please, leave, before—"

There was a knock at the door, and Spencer froze. Who would be knocking on his door at this time of night? And what would they say when they saw the half-dressed young woman unchaperoned in his bedchamber?

He groaned; she was ruined. *He* was ruined. There was nothing to be done.

The girl did not make an attempt to hide. In fact, she reached for the door handle—and before Spencer could tell her not to, she threw the door open, and their fate was sealed.

CHAPTER TWENTY-THREE

THE FIGURE ON the other side of the door gasped. "Louisa!"

Forcing one foot in front of the other, Spencer stepped to the side to see who the feminine voice belonged to, and saw the elder Miss Trentbridge, fully clothed and with a shocked expression on her face.

"I was worried when you were not in our room, sister. I had thought to ask if Lord Leighton had seen you, but I did not expect—"

"Miss Trentbridge appears to have wandered into the wrong room. An innocent error, I am sure..." Spencer said, his voice weary. Did he expect the young lady before him to believe that nothing had happened, when her sister was half-dressed in a single man's bedchamber?

Or was she party to whatever this ridiculous scheme was?

"My lord, you know it is not acceptable for you to be alone with my sister. Why, anything could have—"

Spencer was about to defend himself, and the young lady's honor, when heavy footsteps fell in the hall, and his heart dropped.

Another witness was the last thing he needed. He could practically see himself walking reluctantly down the aisle, and waiting for Miss Trentbridge at the altar. Because however irritated he was, and whether or not this was a set up, he knew his stupid code of honor would not allow him to leave the girl ruined and unwed.

But he would try to avoid that at all costs.

He was half-tempted to pull both women into his bedchamber, so the approaching guest would not see them—but that would surely only look worse. Two young ladies alone in his room, and at least one of them surely protesting.

How had a perfectly ordinary evening turned into this mess?

"What's the problem here?" a male voice asked, and Spencer didn't know if he was relieved or disappointed that it was James. A friendly face was surely a bonus—but would his friend believe that he had nothing to do with this farce?

"I was looking for my sister," Miss Jennifer Trentbridge said. "And I am afraid I found her in Lord Leighton's room, alone, and dressed...thus..." She let out a half-sob, and Spencer gritted his teeth.

Really, society was ridiculous. That a girl's future would be ruined for being in a room where nothing had happened.

And yet no one would believe that nothing had occurred—that was the problem.

And if the lady had been the one who filled his thoughts, and she had stood before him in a translucent night rail that clung to her curves...

Well, then something would have happened. He knew that without a doubt. Despite the fact that he was broken, despite the fact that he knew he would not be a good husband to her, he did not think he could resist the woman he wanted above everything else.

His heart ached for her. His body ached for her. That one kiss they had shared had set his blood burning through the body in a way encounters with other women had never done.

But she was not the young lady in the room.

And he had not so much as had an impure thought about Miss Trentbridge.

And yet... Who would believe him?

James's eyebrows knitted together. "That does not sound like Lord Leighton." He looked up at his friend, and Spencer felt hope bloom in his heart. If James believed him, perhaps there was an escape from this mess.

"The girl was in my room when I came upstairs. I have no idea—"

"Were you lost, Miss Louisa?" James asked, offering her an easy out.

"I—" The girl's eyes widened, and then filled with tears, and guilt poked at Spencer's heart.

At the sound of a door closing down the hallway, James stepped forward. The house was certainly active that night. "Let's get to the bottom of this without giving the rest of the guests a show, shall we?" he said, crossing the threshold into Spencer's room.

Miss Jennifer Trentbridge looked scandalized. "Lord Fount! I certainly cannot countenance my sister and I being alone with two gentlemen—"

"I do not wish to see anyone ruined, Miss Trentbridge. But if we stand here much longer, you might very well both be. And perhaps your sister does not mind a quick and arranged marriage, but I rather think you might."

Spencer was quite impressed at how accurately James had read the situation—and by the horrified look on Jennifer Trentbridge's face, she had not thought of this possible consequence of her presence here, and she did not like it.

She smartly stepped into the chamber without further protest, and James shut the door behind her.

"Now, Miss Louisa. Why are you here, and why are you crying?"

Miss Louisa looked to her sister, and then back at the two gentlemen, before letting out a sob. "Oh, Jenny, I'm sorry. I knew you'd come looking for me, and Lord Leighton's room was the closest, and—"

Miss Jennifer Trentbridge frowned. "What do you mean? Why are you here? Did Lord Leighton proposition you? Or—"

"I did nothing of the kind," Spencer insisted. "All I want is to go to bed, *alone*, and forget this evening ever happened."

"Now, Spencer, the girl is upset," James said, with more patience than Spencer could summon. "Why did you come here?"

She flushed red, and looked to the floor, and then mumbled out a long sentence without really taking a breath. "Lord Leighton seemed so nice, and kind and I thought if Jenny found me in his room, in my night rail, then he would have to marry me, and…"

Spencer gritted his teeth to avoid letting out an irritated growl. Just as he'd thought—the chit was trying to trap him.

He felt sorry for her clear misery, but he did not like being maneuvered.

"Why would you do such a thing?" her sister asked, saving James the need to continue his interrogation.

"Because…because they're going to marry me off to Mr. Jenkins," she said with a sob.

"Our cousin? No, I am sure Mama was joking, she is not—"

Miss Louisa sniffed and shook her head. "Before we came here, she told me that if I was unwed by the end of the year, I would be marrying him. You know the estate is entailed on him, and if I marry him…well, it will become mine too. And then our children's… She believes you have a better chance of a good match than I do, so she wants me to marry him."

"But the man is a bore!" the elder Miss Trentbridge said, louder than Spencer would have liked, considering he did not wish anyone to know there were two unwed misses in his bedchamber. "And thrice your age."

"I know. So I thought…" She looked up at Spencer, tears and despair in her eyes. "I'm sorry, Lord Leighton. I thought… I thought you would do the right thing, and you might save me from my fate. Tricking you was wrong, I am sorry, I just…"

"Didn't know what to do," James finished. "We understand, Miss Trentbridge. And, assuming we can all keep this to ourselves, there is no harm done."

Miss Trentbridge let out a sob. Of course, for her, the harm was done already—if she did not find a husband, she would have to marry the man she despised.

It was almost enough to make Spencer offer her marriage. He hated to see a woman so trapped, so alone in the world, so desperate.

And yet… He knew he could not tie himself to a woman he could never love, to save her from a man she did not love. He hadn't even been able to tie himself to the woman he *did* love, to save her from a similar fate.

"Of course, this will not leave this room," Miss Jennifer Trentbridge assured them. "Lord Leighton, Lord Fount, I can only apologize for my sister's poor judgment and hope you will not hold it against her."

"Of course," James said with a smooth bow, altogether more polite and attentive than Spencer could be in that moment. "Let me make sure the coast is clear, ladies, and you can return to your rooms with no one the wiser."

When they were gone, Spencer sat down on the end of his bed and took a deep breath. That had been close. Far too close. If anyone but James had stumbled across them, or if Miss Louisa had not had an attack of conscience and admitted to her scheme, he could very well be betrothed at this very moment. And that would surely have been a disaster—for both himself, and for Miss Trentbridge, when she realized what she had married. A man who jumped at loud noises. A man who could not look to the future. A man who spent every night trapped in a world of nightmares that he could never escape.

She was better off with the aged, boring gentleman she was to be affianced to.

The door, which James had left ajar, closed, making Spencer jump and then hate himself for doing so. But it was only James, with that easy smile on his face.

"I'm going to go to bed—but I thought you might need some of this first," he said, holding up a silver hip flask that he was rarely without. He handed it to Spencer, who took it gratefully. A large swig of the port inside was what he needed to reset his mind.

"Well, that was a turn up for the books," James said when Spencer had not said anything, but had simply tipped back the hip flask once more.

"Indeed," Spencer finally said. "I suspected she was interested in me, but I did not think she would plan a stunt like this…"

James whistled. "Nor I. She must be really desperate, if she would go to such lengths." He tutted and shook his head. "I know we men are always trying to avoid getting tied down—look at Timothy, for God's sake. Betrothed all this time and still not wishing to set a date. And yet we have so much more choice than the ladies do… Especially those who still need their parents' permission to wed."

Spencer nodded. He did not disagree with his friend's assessment of the plight of unwed young ladies—but right now, he was rather irritated at the trap he had almost been caught in.

"And you have no interest in marrying the girl at all?" James asked, taking back his flask and finishing the contents. "She's an attractive woman, and she'll have been raised for such a position in society…"

"No," Spencer said without needing to think. "No interest."

"Because you do not wish to wed?"

"Because I do not wish to wed…" Spencer began, and then added the word that was on his tongue, even though he knew it would invite questions, "…her."

"Ah," James said, his eyes lighting up. "So there *is* someone you would happily be tied to for the rest of your life."

Spencer closed his eyes and groaned. "Perhaps, not that I wish to discuss this. But I am not fit to be a husband—whether to a girl I wish to wed or one I do not."

"Stuff and nonsense," James said with a loud tut. "That's a story you've told yourself, Spencer, and it's not true."

He had not shared this particular opinion before, and so no one had ever refuted it—but he was shocked at how quickly

James dismissed it.

"It is true," he said, twisting his hands together. "You know how broken I am, after the war. After losing…Jack. After everything."

James narrowed his eyes and pursed his lips. "You may not be the same man as before, but you are not broken. You have a life to live, a title to pass on, and you cannot spend the rest of your life feeling guilty that you survived and your brother, God rest his soul, did not."

Spencer sucked in a deep breath as James's words sank in. He was not speaking harshly, but plainly, and in a way no one had ever spoken to Spencer before.

"I don't feel…" he began before trailing off. Because, of course, his friend was right. He *did* feel guilty for surviving.

He thought he ought to.

But James, apparently, did not.

James put the hip flask back inside his jacket pocket and moved to the door. "Just think on it, Spencer. No one wants to see you miserable for the rest of your days—and I know your brother wouldn't have wanted that, either."

Spencer simply nodded, feeling too overcome by emotion for words.

James moved to the door but paused with his hand on the knob. He peered over his shoulder at him. "And even with what I've said, even if you would be the perfect husband…you have no interest in Miss Louisa, correct?"

Spencer looked at him. "No interest, whatsoever," he confirmed, his voice a little croaky.

He was relieved when his friend left him to return to his own chamber. When he had first come up to his bedchamber, he had thought he would fall straight to sleep. Then the near-disastrous events of the night had delayed his slumber by more than an hour—so when he climbed into bed, sleep did not come.

Instead Spencer found himself picturing the woman he wished to marry—in another life, another world, where such a thing might be possible.

Because even if he wasn't broken beyond repair, which he still believed he was, it was too late. Lady Beatrix was betrothed.

CHAPTER TWENTY-FOUR

"I TRUST," AUNT Elspeth said as Beatrix took her leave, "that you will continue to follow the sensible path which you have begun to follow, and not veer off it on some childish whim."

It took a lot of effort for Beatrix to keep her face impassive as she nodded. "Thank you for your counsel, Aunt."

"And set the wedding date sooner rather than later. I shall not be able to attend, of course, but write to me and tell me as soon as you are wed. Your future will be all the safer with that wedding band on your finger."

"Yes, Aunt. I shall write soon. Make sure you rest and stay warm."

"I am perfectly healthy," her aunt said in a tone even more irritable than the one she usually employed. Beatrix wished to point out that if she were perfectly healthy, she would be able to travel for the wedding of her niece, or would have come to visit her niece in mourning—but she did not.

She had no intention of bringing the wedding forward. She would remain in mourning for as long as she could, and Thomas had agreed to wait.

It was with a heavy heart that she climbed back into the carriage, where Jemima was already waiting. She was not sad to be leaving Aunt Elspeth; she had not found the solace with her relative which she had hoped. But leaving her aunt meant returning to London, to Thomas, to everything she had hoped from which she might find an escape.

And yet there was no escape. Her aunt had merely confirmed that marrying Thomas was the best, and indeed her only, option.

She wished the thought didn't fill her with such misery.

"Are you well, my lady?" Jemima asked as the coach rattled along the road, through the foggy countryside.

Beatrix sighed. "Physically, yes. But my heart aches…"

Jemima reached out and squeezed her hand. They had often overstepped the boundaries between servant and mistress, and Beatrix welcomed the comfort. There was no one else in the world to comfort her.

"All will be well, my lady."

"I do not know how it can be," Beatrix said with a sigh. "If I wed Thomas, then I am secure, and my children will inherit everything Papa built. But I will be married to a man…a man I do not really know." *A man I am wary of,* she added in her head. *A man I do not think I can love.*

"And if you do not marry him?" Jemima prompted.

"Then I will leave with nothing," Beatrix said with a sigh. "And will have to hope I can find paid employment, or someone else to marry me…or I will be homeless. There is no one who will take me in." And of course, her loyal maid would likely too be out of work and homeless, for she could not pay for a maid herself if she left with nothing.

What could her maid say to comfort her? There was only one logical choice. She just needed to ignore the silly romantic part of her heart that wanted a different man.

Because he didn't want her. Not as a wife. And there was no use pretending otherwise.

WHEN SPENCER JOINED the rest of the house party for a late breakfast, he was rather surprised to see Miss Louisa with a bright smile on her face and a sparkle in her eyes. There was a lot of chatter in the room, but he presumed it could not be about the debacle the previous evening—because if it had been, she surely would not have been smiling.

He took his seat and glanced around at the excited company. He was not one to pick up on the subtleties of society normally, but this was too obvious even for him to miss.

"Leighton!" Montgomery said, his booming voice filling the room. "Have you heard the happy news?"

Spencer shook his head, bemused. "I'm afraid I have not."

"Well, this little house party will be ending in rather a romantic air!"

Spencer felt his pulse quicken. This surely had nothing to do with him. He had not agreed to any of the ridiculousness the night before.

"Oh?" he said as calmly as he could, raising an eyebrow.

"Yes! Miss Louisa Trentbridge—"

His heart began to thud harder than it ought to. No. He could not marry her. He could not.

"Has this very morning become betrothed to Lord Fount."

Spencer's jaw dropped and his eyes darted to James—who looked both happy and a little awkward at meeting Spencer's eye.

"Well, my congratulations," Spencer said when he could speak again.

"And not long after, Miss Jennifer Trentbridge agreed to become my wife, also."

"Goodness!" Spencer said, although a much stronger word, not suitable for polite company, had initially come to mind. "What a…busy morning. Congratulations."

The excitable chatter bubbled up again as Spencer helped himself to some fruit, feeling rather relieved. Two betrothals, and neither involved him. And he was pleased too, that in spite of her scheming, that Miss Louisa had found a way to avoid the marriage she had been dreading.

It had all worked out for the best.

And yet, as they promenaded around the gardens on this their final afternoon of the house party, which the sun had kindly decided to shine upon, for some reason he did not feel full of joy.

That was not unusual for him, but he was surprised to find the feeling that welled up inside him as he watched the two happy couples strolling arm in arm was…jealousy.

Not for either of the women. He had been honest with James: he had no desire to wed Miss Louisa. And though her sister was equally pretty, he had no wish to further his connection with her, either.

No, he envied the ease of the relationship. The way they seemed so happy and confident in one another's company. The fact that they would have someone by their side, for the rest of their lives.

He didn't want to be alone, forever.

He didn't think he could be a husband…but he didn't want to be alone.

CHAPTER TWENTY-FIVE

THE GRIEF IN Beatrix's heart did not lessen after a month, and neither did living with her betrothed get any easier. She had arrived home to find everything as she had left it, and two days later, Thomas's sister arrived—making their living together acceptable in society's eyes.

If Beatrix had hoped she would be an ally, she was sorely mistaken.

"Beatrix, allow me to present my sister, Sarah," Thomas had said on the day they'd first met. He'd dropped the 'Lady' from her name without asking, but she supposed it was only right, since they were to be wed.

She'd beamed at the lady before her, who was a few years her senior, and tried to push her sadness from her mind, for she sincerely wished to have a good relationship with her new family.

"Mrs. Jones will suffice," Sarah said, smoothing her skirt and looking Beatrix up and down.

"Oh. Yes. Of course. It's a pleasure to meet you, Mrs. Jones." Shocked by her abruptness, Beatrix took a step back, unsure how to react. "Thank you for coming to stay. I am sure you are very busy…"

"Sarah has three children, all boys," Thomas informed her proudly. All Beatrix could wonder was how she had left her children, presumably with their father and a maid or nanny, for three whole months in order to chaperone her brother and his betrothed.

"Is she in trouble then?" Sarah asked her brother. "Is that why you're marrying? Waiting makes no sense—"

It took Beatrix a moment to decipher the meaning behind Sarah's question, and when she did, she was outraged.

"I most certainly am not!" she declared, when Thomas seemed slow to inform his sister that there was nothing improper about their relationship.

"Sarah, as I told you, Beatrix was the daughter of my predecessor. She will make an excellent countess."

Sarah sniffed. "If you say so."

Beatrix did not think she had ever encountered such an unpleasant woman, and when the butler Samson suggested he show Mrs. Jones to her room to rest after her journey—although it had only been from the other side of London—Beatrix was quick to agree.

"Is that what people think about us?" Beatrix hissed, incensed. Until this point she had ignored any rudeness or lack of tact from Thomas, choosing to believe it was all unintended. But to have her honor called into question, when she was in mourning and had agreed to marry this man with no real desire for him, was just too much.

"Calm yourself, Beatrix," Thomas said, as though he was speaking to an over-excited infant. "My sister is merely blunt. She knows I have not wed up until now, and simply wonders why I have now chosen to do so. Remember she is doing us a great favor by staying here, so that we can wait to be wed as *you* have insisted."

Beatrix felt her cheeks flame red—both at the earlier suggestion of her already carrying Thomas's child, and the way he was admonishing her.

"Well. I am glad she is here for propriety's sake," she eventually said, although in her head she wished that his sister had never come.

Almost a month later, the relationship with the two soon-to-be sisters-in-law had not much improved. Sarah had kept herself to herself, choosing new furnishings for rooms that Thomas had given her permission to redecorate, and complaining when Beatrix was in her way reading or sewing.

Beatrix wanted to cry at the way her beloved home was being criticized, and how Sarah planned to redecorate her beloved parlor without even asking.

The house belonged to Thomas, yes, and he had every right to ask his sister's opinion on the furnishings. But even if Beatrix had not spent her childhood in that house, she would have thought he might value her opinion, as his future wife, over that of a sister he'd even admitted himself whom he had not seen for years prior to this visit.

And yet she did not feel she could say anything. Day after day she tried to fill her time and her thoughts and not burst into tears, in the hopes that things would be better once she and Thomas were wed, and she was truly the lady of the house.

But what if things are worse?

The question plagued her often, and she did not have an answer for it. Her mind occasionally wandered to that incredible kiss with Lord Leighton, but whenever that happened she forced herself to think of something else. Not because she regretted it, but because she doubted she would ever feel that way about anyone else, especially Thomas—and it hurt to think about what could have been, if Lord Leighton had not gone to war after they had danced, and had instead called on her as he had vowed to in Vauxhall Gardens.

SPENCER KNEW HE had been drinking too much. For the last few weeks, he had spiraled downward into a state of misery that rivaled how he had been when he had first returned from France.

The nights were worse than ever. And during the day, he had nothing to occupy him. He knew he ought to go to the country because he had work to do there and far more to keep him occupied, but he could not bring himself to leave.

Nor could he bring himself to go and stay with James, as he had been invited to do. He did not think his friend would accept his misery without questioning it, and Spencer did not want to discuss why he was drinking so much. Besides, the invitation had been extended before James had proposed marriage to Miss Louisa Trentbridge—and so, perhaps it no longer stood.

He still did not wholly understand what had happened there. Had James offered marriage out of pity for the girl? Or did he truly harbor feelings for her?

Spencer hoped it was the latter, and hoped to find out the truth as soon as he saw his friend again.

Drinking so much was partly so that he could sleep better, in the hopes that the nightmares would not come—although a month of trying this theory had proven that it did not work. But more than that, it was to block out the terrible feelings of regret he felt every time he thought of Lady Beatrix.

It was ridiculous. They had danced a few times, held hands twice, kissed once. Granted, it was more than he would have ever done with any other well-born lady, but it was surely not enough to send him into this state of misery.

But he wanted to be the man who was marrying her. He hated the thought of her marrying the new Lord Haxbury. She had looked so lost and broken herself when he had visited, and when she had come to see him, he had thought there was another reason than to inform him of her betrothal.

But it was too late now. Everyone knew that they were to be married, and he was not going to interrupt her happiness to what—offer marriage to himself? He didn't even think he was capable of that. And if he was, it would be terribly unfair of him to tie her to a broken man who could not sleep through the night without nightmares, when she had a chance of real happiness before her.

But knowing all of that did not diminish his misery, and so he tried to dull it with drink. Sometimes at home alone in his library, and sometimes, when the looks from his valet and butler were becoming too judgmental, he came to the club alone and sat in the corner he had always chosen with Timothy and James, watching people going about their lives with the decanter before him.

The day that the new Lord Haxbury chose to enter Spencer's club was one of the days when the looks at home had become too judgmental.

Spencer didn't notice him right away; his attention was on a group playing cards, where the stakes had become ridiculously high. They were foolish to gamble with such large figures, but there was still rather a vicarious thrill in watching it unfold.

When he did notice Haxbury, he froze, not wishing for the man to recognize him. But then, why would he? They had only met once. He had been a mere inconvenience in Lord Haxbury's day, whereas his image had been seared into Spencer's mind because he was marrying the woman that, in another life, Spencer would have made his wife.

His attention drawn away from the cards, he watched the new earl as he bought a drink and then got chatting to a few of the other patrons who were milling around the bar. Ever so slowly, so that he was not noticed, he edged his chair nearer so that he could hear the conversation. It was stupid, but he could not resist.

He could not have known that that simple action would change his life forever.

"Ah, so you're the new Lord Haxbury," a balding gentleman said, offering his hand to shake. "We wondered when we'd be seeing you about town. Didn't know if you'd already left for the country."

"Not yet. I'm staying in the city until after I'm wed—and then, yes, I rather think we will retire to the country. I don't see any need for the new countess to return to the city..."

The suggestive tone to his voice made Spencer ball up his hands into fists, but he got his anger under control and did not rise. He did not like Beatrix being spoken of in such a way, but it was hardly uncommon amongst the men. And he was nothing to her. If he jumped up and defended her honor, he would only make a fool of himself, and perhaps ruin Beatrix's happiness.

"Oh yes, I did hear that you were betrothed to old Haxbury's daughter. Congratulations," a younger fellow further away from Spencer said. It seemed like most of the patrons were interested in this new earl, and he soon had quite a crowd around him.

Spencer knew he ought to go home, but he stayed where he was, not drinking, not moving, just listening to the increasingly drunken comments that passed between the gentlemen—if they could be called that.

"No, no, no. I assure you, gentlemen, any rumors you've heard about my betrothed are wholly untrue. She is the epitome of a virgin bride. A little cold and unfeeling, as these untouched women so often are, but once we're married, I'll take her in hand and warm her up."

The men around him laughed, but Spencer simply saw red.

"She may hold me at arm's length now, but once the vows have been said, she will do her duty with enthusiasm, I assure you."

"How dare you?" He jumped out of his seat at the same time shouting, and it took the drunken lords a while to even register that he was speaking to them—well, to one of them in particular.

"You are marrying one of the best women of the *ton* and you dare speak of her like this. I cannot bear to hear it."

Lord Haxbury turned and narrowed his eyes. "Oh. Lord…Laysbury, wasn't it?"

"Leighton," Spencer corrected through gritted teeth.

"Well, Lord Leighton, if you do not like the topic of conversation, might I suggest that you leave? I rather suspected you were angling for an affair with my soon-to-be wife, but I assure you, the rumors of any liaison between her and a notorious rake are false, and she is mine now."

Lord Haxbury's words only served to incense Spencer more.

How dare he suggest that Spencer had been trying to lure Beatrix into some sort of immoral relationship? Without even thinking about it, Spencer found his hands on the lapels of Lord Haxbury's jacket, and he pulled him to his feet and landed a blow on his chin before he even realized what was happening.

"How dare you!" Haxbury roared, once he had recovered from the blow. "I am the Earl of Haxbury, and you have no right to—"

"And *I* am the Marquess of Leighton, and I will defend the lady's honor."

They were torn apart from each other before Haxbury managed to land a single blow, but there was no way that Spencer was going to walk away after hearing him speak so foully.

"Name your second," he found himself shouting, without thinking of the consequences. "I will not listen to the lady's good name besmirched. We duel at dawn—unless you are willing to rescind your comments and apologize to the lady in question."

"I'll see you at dawn," the new earl spat.

CHAPTER TWENTY-SIX

THE FIRST THING Beatrix knew of the events at the club was when she was startled awake by the front door, which happened to be directly below her chamber, being slammed shut. The house seemed to shake for a moment, and she sat up in bed, her heart racing in panic. *What on earth is going on?*

When she heard heavy footsteps on the stairs, she wondered if she ought to defend herself, in case it was an intruder or a burglar, and so she dashed to her dresser to find her sewing scissors. They weren't particularly sharp, but they were surely better than nothing.

In the dim light of the moon, which peeked into her room through a gap in the curtains, it was hard to find them, and before she was able, her bedroom door flew open.

She jumped and gasped at the sight of Thomas in the doorway, holding a candle, his face furious.

"Thomas! Are you well? It is very late—"

"What relationship do you have with Lord Leighton?" he asked, slurring slightly. A shiver went down her spine. She and Thomas's relationship so far had been awkward, but not particularly contentious—mainly because Beatrix never argued back. But now he was storming into her bedchamber at past midnight, when she was in only her nightdress, demanding an answer to a ridiculous question.

"We are friends," she said, the irritation rising up her in voice.

"You met him when he came to give his condolences, remember? I do not know what has prompted this, but you should not be in my bedchamber, so please—"

She squeaked as he reached out and grabbed her forearm, dragging her towards him. His grip was tight enough that she thought it might bruise, and for the first time she was scared of the man.

"I have defended your honor tonight," he said in a low whisper, the alcohol on his breath making her want to gag. "Do you know what they say about you and a man called Ambrose Trentham?"

Beatrix blanched. She had not expected to hear his name tonight, from Thomas's lips. She knew that her relationship with the notorious rake had caused whispers among the ton—but nothing beyond a few kisses had ever occurred between them.

It seemed rather unfair that his reputation with women was still impacting her, long after he was dead. And she struggled to understand how this was related to Lord Leighton, whose name still set her heart racing.

Surely Thomas couldn't know about the kiss?

"We were betrothed, I've told you that. Years ago. But he died in a duel."

"No one believes you could have associated with such a cad and remained virtuous." He squeezed her arm so hard that tears began to well in her eyes. He was clearly drunk, and angry, and all she could think was to placate him and get him out of her chamber.

"I swear to you, on—on my father's grave, that nothing happened between Ambrose and me."

That seemed to mollify him a little, and his grip on her arm loosened. "Well. That is what I told them. But you understand that I expect my wife to have a spotless reputation, do you not?"

"Of—of course, Thomas," Beatrix stuttered. How could she marry this man?

And then his grip on her arm tightened once more. "And

Leighton? He is not some betrothed from years ago. He is here now, and he has far more interest in you than he should, interfering busybody."

What happened tonight? Beatrix wondered desperately, as she tried to twist her arm from his grip to no avail. Had he seen Lord Leighton? What had been said? Thomas surely didn't know about the kiss, or it would have been mentioned already… "We are friends. He knew my father. That is all."

"You swear?"

"I swear," she said, holding back tears and hoping God would forgive her for swearing when she felt something towards Lord Leighton that did not belong in friendship.

Her feelings didn't matter now. She had agreed to marry Thomas, and she had nowhere to go if she did not.

She was truly trapped.

"You do not need male friends," he said, letting her arm go suddenly. It ached as the blood returned to its normal flow, and she held back tears. She would not cry in front of him. "I will not have you bringing shame on the Haxbury name."

Beatrix shook her head, not trusting herself to speak. She had been a daughter of the Earl of Haxbury her entire life, and yet this man thought he could lecture her on not shaming his precious new title?

If she hadn't been scared of him, she would have been furious. But instead she kept her feelings inside, and when he finally left, stumbling down the corridor, she closed her door and barricaded it with her chair.

And then she let the tears fall, as the reality of the situation sank in. Not only was she marrying a man she barely knew, a man she did not care for—she was also marrying a man of whom she was afraid.

And she had no idea how to get out of it without ending up living on the streets.

SPENCER SAT ON a bench in Putney Heath, a pistol in his hands, and waited for dawn.

He had not slept all night. What was the point? He would only have nightmares, and this day would quite possibly be his very last on Earth.

He watched the sun begin to rise as he waited for the man he had called out to arrive.

His hands shook to hold a pistol once more, and he knew that as soon as one of them discharged their weapon, he would be right back on the field in France, watching his brother die. And yet, this was different. He couldn't find it in himself to care that much that his life might soon be taken by the new Earl of Haxbury.

He had been defending Beatrix's honor, and he would do so again, no matter the consequences. Even now, in the darkness before dawn, he could not bring himself to regret his actions.

And perhaps he would not die. Perhaps he would be victorious, killing Haxbury, or at least drawing blood. He did not want to take another man's life, especially in such circumstances and not as a consequence of war, but equally, he could not stand by and watch the woman who had filled his dreams marry such a scoundrel. She deserved better. Not that he thought he was the right man to marry her, but Lord Haxbury certainly wasn't.

He just hoped that this duel would put an end to their marriage plans.

As the sky began to lighten, he prayed to a God he wasn't sure he believed in anymore. And then he spoke to the ghosts who had haunted his dreams, who had affected his decisions every day since they had passed. "I'm sorry, Father. Jack. I'm sorry I could not be the marquess that you were, that you would have been, brother. But if we meet again this morning, please know that I tried my best. In everything."

He did not have a second. There was no man in town that he could possibly ask to do such a thing. But he would happily stand opposite Haxbury with no witnesses, no adjudicator—to ensure Lady Beatrix's honor was restored.

CHAPTER TWENTY-SEVEN

T HE NEXT MORNING, after very little sleep, Beatrix stayed in her room. She did not wish to see Thomas or Sarah. She had spent all night trying to come up with a plan, and the only thing she was sure of was that she could not marry a man who would treat her like that.

She could break the engagement. He could ruin her reputation, but from what he had said, it was already pretty damaged. So now she just needed somewhere to live, some way to earn money—something which she would have already secured if he hadn't proposed marriage. She'd thought it was the easiest option. But it wasn't. And keeping her home wasn't worth being with a man like that.

When Jemima came to help her dress, Beatrix let her in and then barricaded the door behind her.

"Milady?" Jemima asked with a frown. "What's wrong?"

"I—" Her voice shook, but she did not want to lie to Jemima. Besides, she needed some support, and who else did she have in this world?

"I cannot marry him," she whispered. "I have seen what kind of man he is, and I cannot go through with it."

"Well, thank heavens for that," Jemima said with a broad grin.

"You don't think I should marry him?"

"Of course not! Oh, I understand why you feel—felt—it was

the best decision. But pardon me for being frank, I cannot see you being happy with him, milady."

Tears sprang to Beatrix's eyes at this confirmation of her fears. "But if I go… I have nowhere. Nothing. I cannot take you with me, Jemima, when I have no money to employ you. I—"

"Hush, milady," Jemima said, placing a hand on her arm soothingly. Beatrix winced; the area was already showing the green of a bruise that she was sure would darken later.

"What happened to your arm?"

"Nothing…" She did not know why she lied, other than feeling like she was more at risk the more she shared. But Jemima could read the fear in her eyes, she was sure.

"Well. Never mind about not being able to take me with you. I will always be your friend—and I'm capable of finding myself work, so don't you worry about me. Do not tie yourself to a man for the rest of your life out of fear. You will have to share his bed, bear his children, grow old with him."

"And I cannot."

"No. So what is your plan?"

"I…" Who could she turn to for help? Perhaps she could run north to Aunt Esther's house. But she had always gone on about not bringing shame on the family name, and she had made it very clear that Beatrix needed to marry Thomas. When faced with the reality of her penniless niece on her doorstep, would she turn her away? Beatrix had never known her aunt to change her mind. And if she did not wish to associate with her, then Beatrix would be poor and alone in a strange place…

At least London held more employment opportunities, or ways of discovering them at any rate.

There was only one person she thought she could ask for advice. One friend who would side with her over Thomas. But if her betrothed found out she had been visiting him, she would be in an even worse situation. Indeed, it was her previous interaction with Leighton that has seemed to incite his wrath.

And yet, she had to try.

"I need to go out, Jemima. Without anyone knowing. Can you find out where Thomas and Sarah are, and put about that I'm unwell and staying in bed?" She wasn't sure such news would keep Thomas from her chamber, if he really wished to enter, but it was the best cover she could think of.

"Of course, milady."

Jemima returned quicker than Beatrix had expected. She was trying to get herself into a simple day dress when her maid returned and, ever the professional, began to fasten the dress as she relayed the information she had been sent to acquire.

"Lord Haxbury is still abed. Apparently he had a terrible headache, and his valet does not expect him to be up for several hours."

The headache served him right. Beatrix smiled at both the justice and the fact that he wouldn't notice her slipping out. "And Sarah?"

"Mrs. Jones left to go to the modiste about twenty minutes ago, Samson tells me."

The perfect time, then, for her to slip away. "Do not tell them I've gone out. But if they discover it, please pretend you did not know. I couldn't bear for you to suffer their wrath."

"I can look after myself. You're sure you do not wish me to accompany you?"

"No, thank you. I need to do this alone."

She took off out of the front door, checking behind her continuously, and hurried along the pavements until she reached the house where she hoped some helpful advice lay: the London residence of Lord Leighton.

If it had been improper for her to visit with Jemima, then to do so alone, when her betrothed had all but forbidden it, was downright scandalous—but she couldn't bring herself to care.

In her wildest dreams, she hoped he would offer to marry her, to save her from this mess. But she knew that was unlikely. She just needed him to help her to escape this situation. She would take his money if she had to, because anything was better than staying with Thomas.

Lord Leighton, the man who had filled her dreams since that magical first dance in Vauxhall Gardens, was the only friend she could turn to in order to escape this mess she had got herself into.

She knocked on the door and tried to think of a reason for her visit, should the staff ask. But when the door opened, the butler looked rather ashen faced already.

"I am here to see Lord Leighton," she said, pulling herself up to her full height and pretending like she had every right to be there.

"I'm afraid he is not at home, my lady."

"Oh." For some reason, she had not been expecting that. "Is everything well?"

He dithered for a moment, clearly unsure what he should say, but his concern won out. "He went out in the early hours of the morning, and we have not seen him since. The stable lad said he was going to Putney Heath."

Beatrix's blood ran cold. Putney Heath, at dawn, was well known for being the location of a many an illegal duel, since it was far enough away from the center of the city that the authorities were unlikely to come across it.

It was also the location where Ambrose Trentham, the man she had once planned to marry, had lost his life.

Why would Lord Leighton be there? He surely had no reason to duel anyone. It had to be a coincidence.

She needed to see him, wherever she was. And her fears about his reason for being on Putney Heath—even though it was now late morning, and not dawn—would not subside until she saw him.

"May I borrow his lordship's carriage, in order to fetch him home?" she asked, surprised at her own boldness.

"Of course, my lady. I shall ready it at once."

As the coach rattled out towards Putney Heath, Beatrix thought that the butler must have had the same thoughts as she did about Lord Leighton, else he surely would not have allowed her to have the carriage without any protest. She hoped that Thomas's anger the previous night was not related to Lord Leighton's disappearance. But he *had* mentioned him…

Yet, Thomas was at home suffering from the effects of over-imbibing, she told herself. There was no need to worry.

Except that she hadn't actually seen him since he had stumbled into her room in the middle of the night. What if they had got into a fight? What if…

She couldn't contemplate the possibilities. She wished she were riding, so she could urge the horse faster, but instead she had to accept the slow speed of the carriage, and hope she would not find blood had been shed upon the grass of Putney Heath when she arrived.

After what felt like hours, the coach stopped and she threw the door open, not waiting for the driver to hand her down. She shouted her thanks, lifted her skirts and ran, her eyes scanning the park to see if she could spot either of the men.

If they had gone into the woodland then she would have no hope of finding them. For the moment, her own worries faded away, as the fear that the man she was betrothed to, and the one she was seeking out, had engaged in a deadly duel overwhelmed her.

There were a few people around riding horses or promenading, but no one was screaming and there were no magistrates around. She was sure she was drawing attention to herself, a lone woman running through the park, but she had to find them.

She had to find Lord Leighton.

And then she saw him. Sitting on a bench, his outline seeming to shake. When she got closer, she saw he had a pistol in his hands, and his body was indeed trembling.

"Lord Leighton?" she said softly, not wanting to surprise him and end up with an accidental shot going off.

He looked up, and the horror in his eyes was apparent for her to see.

"Are you well?"

He blinked, as though he did not understand the question, and she took two steps closer. "May I sit down?"

He did not nod, but he did not shake his head either, and she took it as a sign that he wasn't vehemently opposed to her presence.

CHAPTER TWENTY-EIGHT

LORD HAXBURY HAD not appeared at dawn, and although that hour was well past, Spencer could not move from the bench, the pistol in his shaking hands.

He had called for the duel. And he was fairly sure he would have seen it through, even with the images of the battlefield filling his head.

But now he could not escape the past.

The arrival of Lady Beatrix made no sense, but his mind would not work well enough for him to ask her why she was there. Perhaps she knew of the duel, and was there to beg for her betrothed's life.

But the man did not deserve her.

"Please put the pistol down, Lord Leighton," she said, gently placing her hands upon his, not seeming to care that they were in a public place. Her voice sounded scared, and it cut through the haze, giving him the strength to push the pistol to one side.

"What are you doing here?" she asked.

"What are *you* doing here?" he responded, not wanting to admit to the duel without knowing what she knew.

"I need your help," she said, and her blue eyes were wide and desperate. "You said if I needed anything…and I do. I went to your house, and they said you were here. They were worried…"

Spencer nodded and glanced up at the sun. It was surely approaching midday, and he had left well before dawn. No wonder the staff were worried.

"What's wrong?" he asked, finally gaining some control over his senses. "Of course, I will help, if I can…"

Tears filled her eyes, and he wanted to hold her, but he could not. Instead he contented himself with the fact that her hands were still atop his. "I cannot marry him," she whispered.

"Haxbury?"

She nodded. "He is not…the man I thought he was. I cannot tie myself to him for the rest of my days."

He was not good enough for her, that was true—but Spencer had no idea what he could do to help her. Their betrothal had been publicly announced; to break it off would cause scandal. And although he thought she could live with that, the reason she had said yes to the marriage in the first place was surely for the financial stability. She had said no to any money Spencer had offered her—and he could not offer her enough to set her up for the rest of her life, anyway.

"Please, help me," she begged.

His heart ached to hear her pain, but he had no answers. "I've tried, and I've failed," he said miserably. "I do not know what—"

"Please, I have no one else to turn to. I must get out of that house. I think…" She bit her bottom lip, as though unsure whether she could say the words in her head. "I thought he was a good man. But I do not think he is. I'm scared to stay there."

And hearing the fear in her voice, Spencer thought he would have done anything to make her feel safe. She deserved a life where she felt secure and happy.

"There must be some way," she said, tears beginning to fall. "Something I can do. I refuse to believe this is my only option in life."

"Well…there is only one easy way out of this. You could marry someone else, quickly. It would be scandalous, but you could weather that storm. You're of age, you don't need his permission…and once you were wed, he couldn't touch you."

She squeezed his hands, and the hope in her eyes made him

realize what she was thinking when he spoke those words. It was truly the only answer he could think of to her predicament—but that didn't mean it could be him.

That wasn't what he meant.

"Lady Beatrix…"

She shook her head. "Just Beatrix. Please…"

"Beatrix," he said, swallowing, the air thick with longing and desire and misery. "I'm sure you can find a man—"

"I am unwed at the age of twenty-five, despite having a good name and a moderate dowry," she said with a sigh. "I don't believe I *can* find a man to wed. And in truth, there is only one I want to marry."

His heart felt like it had stopped beating. She couldn't be saying these things. He had known there was a spark between them, but he had thought it was mostly in his own mind. That she wanted to marry Haxbury. That she would never consider…

But no. That was not the reason he had not pursued her. He had not feared rejection; he had known he wasn't good enough.

"It cannot be me, Beatrix," he said, his voice unsteady. "I am a broken man, and you deserve so much more."

"But I don't want more. I want you, Lord Leighton."

Desire flooded his body at her words, and yet still he held back. Moments ago he had been sat shaking with a gun, relieving his worst nightmares on the battlefield in his mind. At night he did so with alarming regularity, waking the household by crying out.

He was not fit to be her husband.

But he didn't say any of that. Instead he said, "Spencer."

Her eyes reflected acknowledgment and perhaps, he imagined, pleasure at being given permission to use his Christian name. "I know you think you are broken. But I will help you heal. We can be happy together, Spencer. I am sure of it."

The pleasure he felt upon hearing her say his name was unexpected, and her sentiment made Spencer felt as though he could breathe again. And even though he could not see how he could possibly deserve the happiness that she was offering, he was not going to let this woman fall into the clutches of a man like Lord Haxbury.

If she was willing to help him heal, he was more than willing to save her from the monster who wished to claim her.

She pulled up the sleeve of her dress, showing an angry-looking bruise on her forearm that sent fury through his body. "This is my future, if I cannot leave *that man*."

He wanted to hunt Haxbury down for daring to lay a hand on her, but right now was not the time. Instead he asked, "You're sure?", giving her one final chance to turn away from him, to find someone else.

But she just smiled, her blue eyes twinkling, the tears no longer rolling down her cheeks and said, "I've been sure ever since that night under the lamps in Vauxhall Gardens."

Without caring that she was still betrothed to another man, or that it was broad daylight, or that they were in a public place, Spencer pulled her close and pressed his lips to hers, his heart bursting with joy.

CHAPTER TWENTY-NINE

O NCE IT WAS decided that they would wed, Spencer took charge—and Beatrix was more than happy to let him. They needed to be married quickly, in case Thomas tried to find her and drag her back. Luckily, with Spencer being a marquess, he could organize a special license without too much difficulty.

"We can wed tomorrow," Spencer said, having parted with a not insignificant amount of money to procure the license. But he didn't hesitate to hand it over; in fact, he seemed rather pleased, something Beatrix couldn't imagine Haxbury doing or being happy about.

In fact, she hadn't seen Lord Leighton—Spencer—smile as much in all the time she'd known him as she'd seen this day.

Beatrix beamed. "Thank you. You are saving me from…a fate I cannot bear to contemplate."

"You don't have to thank me," Spencer said softly, taking her hand. Beatrix felt as though he wanted to say more, but his eyes clouded over, and his mind returned to the practical. "You cannot return home tonight. If Haxbury suspects…"

A shiver ran down Beatrix's spine. She had no wish to see the man again—especially when he might be angry with her. The previous night she had worried he might force himself upon her, and while she hoped that sober, and in the light of day, he would think better of it, she wasn't entirely convinced.

"No."

"It would be inappropriate for you to stay at my home, before we are wed. If any of my staff were to say anything..."

Beatrix did not think she cared much for her reputation now. After all, she'd been seen in a public place holding the hands of a man she was not married to. And kissing him! But, if Spencer cared, then she would too. She didn't want to embarrass him, now he'd agreed to save her, agreed to be her husband. The man she had dreamed about for so many years...She could hardly believe it was happening.

"We should go to an inn," Spencer said decisively. "A little out of the city, so we shan't be found, but close enough for me to return tomorrow to retrieve the license. We can give false names, and Haxbury will never find out."

She hated hearing the name of "Haxbury" spoken with such disdain, even though she felt equal dislike towards the new bearer of the name.

"Of course, Spencer. Whatever you think..."

"I know it's not entirely proper. But I think it's the safest option."

"I trust you."

The smile he gave her made her heart glow. She would happily put her life in his hands and trust that she would be happier for it.

⇶≪⇷

HE STOPPED ASKING her whether she was sure, because she'd insisted she was, and that kiss was all the proof he needed. He hadn't thought she should be tied to a broken man like him—but she knew about his demons, and she still wanted him.

And there was no way he was going to let her fall into the clutches of Haxbury. He didn't know exactly what the man had done to alert Beatrix to his true nature, but Spencer would ensure he never laid a hand on her again.

He did not stop to think about whether he was capable of being her husband. He had to do this—for her. They needed to marry as quickly as possible, and she needed to be kept out of Haxbury's clutches until there was nothing he could do to stop the union.

By the time everything was arranged and a plan made, dusk was upon them. The carriage ride in the hired hack to the inn was quiet, and when they arrived he told Beatrix to follow what he said.

"Do you have any rooms available?" he asked the innkeeper, an elderly man with a missing tooth.

"Yes milord, we've one left. Fine room it is too sir, and a good meal as well…"

He had hoped to procure two rooms, so that Beatrix might have her space on the eve of the wedding, but he did not wish to traipse around inns. As he had been rather reclusive, he did not think it likely that someone would recognize him, but they might recognize Lady Beatrix—and if word got back to Haxbury about her whereabouts, then he might come after her.

And that duel might become a reality.

He was willing to risk his own life to defend Beatrix's honor, even if holding a pistol brought everything rushing back. But if he lost, and died, then she would be alone, defenseless against that monster.

And that wasn't something he was willing to risk.

A maid showed them up to the room, and while she looked surprised at their lack of luggage, she didn't comment. The door closed behind them on the sparse room, furnished with a small table and two chairs in one corner, and a stand and a wash basin in the other. However, it was taken up primarily with a four-poster bed, and Spencer felt his mouth go dry.

He was alone in a bedchamber with the woman whom he wanted more than anything else in the world.

But they were not yet wed.

"I'm sorry there was only one room," he said. "I will sleep on the floor. It's just for tonight, and then—"

"We'll be married tomorrow, Spencer," Beatrix said with a blush, removing her cloak. "I don't think it matters all that much whether we share a room, or a bed, tonight."

Spencer nodded and pulled at his cravat, which suddenly felt too tight. No, he supposed it didn't matter. But it wasn't right for him to ravish her on that four-poster as though she were his new bride, either—even if that was what he ached to do.

He wanted to do this *right*. Even if she was marrying him because she needed to escape her situation. Even if he had only agreed to marry her to save her. She'd said she would help him heal, that they would be happy together, and good Lord he wanted that more than anything.

Even more than he wanted her physically in that moment.

"I have not eaten all day," she said softly. "Perhaps we could go down to eat?"

"We should eat in here, to make sure you are not seen. But yes, I will go and ask for a meal to be sent up." He hadn't eaten either, but until that moment, he hadn't realized how hungry he was. The fear, emotion, and adrenaline of the day had quite wiped it from his mind. The only hunger he'd thought of was his desire for her—and that needed to be ignored until they were wed.

Wed. She was going to be his wife. His partner, his other half, and everything would be permitted.

He would most likely have those children to inherit the title that he had thought he would never have.

She'd changed his life in an instant, and he hadn't stopped to think about it. It was rather overwhelming, and his breathing became short.

"Spencer?"

"Sorry. Yes, a meal. I'll go down now. I'll be back shortly."

Beatrix nodded. "And you should probably send word to your staff that you're well, too. Not where we are, of course, but…they were worried."

"Yes, yes, thank you," he said, hurrying from the room. Once the door was closed he leaned back against the solid wood and took a deep, steadying breath.

Before that day, he had not thought that anyone would worry about him if he disappeared.

Could he do this? Be Beatrix's husband? Lay next to her every night? She would find out about his nightmares, there was no doubting that. Probably that very night.

He hurried down the stairs, pushing the fears away. He hadn't thought he would be a good soldier, until he'd had no choice. And while he hoped marriage wouldn't leave him broken like war had, now that it was happening, he would have to find the strength to be a good husband.

Because Beatrix needed him.

With the meals ordered and a note sent to his London home, reassuring them he was safe, but with no details that could lead to him being found, he hurried back upstairs. To the room where she was waiting for him.

She was sitting on the bed, looking nervous. Did she think he wouldn't act as a gentleman?

He took a seat on one of the hard wooden chairs and tried to smile. "So. Tomorrow. After we are married... I think it will be safe to go back to your home, and retrieve your possessions. He may argue over anything of value..."

"I don't care," Beatrix said instantly. "There are a few personal trinkets I would appreciate, as they hold memories of my mother and father... But he can keep the rest. I thought keeping my home and my things and my position was worth... Well, was worth the sacrifice of marrying a man I do not like, let alone...respect." Her teeth worried at her bottom lip. He recognized it as something he'd seen her do before and it occurred to him he'd have the pleasure of watching her perform that delicate and somehow appealing action for the rest of his life. His heart warmed. "But nothing is worth being married to the wrong man. There are no right reasons..."

"No," Spencer agreed. "And trinkets or not, you will not lose your memories. And I can afford to look after you properly, do not fear."

"I'm not worried," she said, and her easy smile made his heart jump. Could he really be meant for someone so light and happy and pure?

"And tonight," he said, feeling he needed to warn her. Her cheeks instantly flushed red, and he hurried on, keen that she not misunderstand his intentions. "I must warn you…since the war, I have rather vivid nightmares. I have been told that I shout out. I don't want to alarm you…"

"Thank you for warning me," she said, with no hint of fear. "Have you found anything that helps them?"

He shook his head. "I had hoped…I know it is ridiculous, but it was my reason for being in Bath, to take the waters. I hoped they might treat the way I react to loud noises, and the night terrors. But alas…"

He didn't want her to see him as a weak man, but he wanted her to know the truth of the man she was marrying. He wasn't trapping her into this marriage. She knew his faults, and she was the one who had said she was sure.

"Perhaps if you spoke about your time in France?" she suggested. "It may help to get it out, rather than it plaguing you at night."

He shook his head. "I don't like to talk about it."

She nodded. "Well, I shan't run from the room if you start shouting in the night."

WHEN HE HAD spoken of that night, she had thought he wanted to discuss the marital act. She wished she knew more of what it entailed, but Jemima had never been very forthcoming, and without her mother, there was no one who felt it was important to impart those details.

And no one, aside from Spencer and the bishop, knew that she would be wed by the following day.

She initially thought they should wait until their wedding night—and she could admit to herself that it was partly because she was nervous, and keen to put off the moment for as long as possible.

But while he had been gone, she'd wondered if she was being silly. She had enjoyed kissing him, however brief it had been. And morally, she could not see that it mattered all that much whether the marriage was consummated the day before or the night of the ceremony. And they were alone in an inn, where everyone already thought they were married…

They sat at the small table in the corner of the room and ate the meal, which was a perfectly serviceable stew. Beatrix was surprised at how famished she was, in spite of her nerves. Nerves about being alone with Spencer, about marrying him, and about Thomas finding them before the vows were said.

If he did find her, would he drag her home and force her to marry him? She was old enough to say no, but she knew well enough that there were men of the cloth who would turn a blind eye to an unwilling, or even unconscious, bride. She'd heard horror stories whispered among the staff, when they'd thought she wasn't listening.

And after the previous night, she wouldn't put anything past Thomas.

She wasn't sure why he was so keen to marry her, when he didn't seem to like her very much. It wasn't like it was for monetary gain, for he was the one who would pay her dowry, if he chose to do so. It was saving him that sum, she reasoned—but it was a small amount compared to the fortune he had inherited.

She supposed it wouldn't look very good, with their betrothal public knowledge, that she had reneged. Perhaps it would damage his male pride. But once the choice was out of his hands, he would have no option but to accept it.

And tomorrow, she would be Lady Beatrix Leighton. The thought sent a shiver down her spine. She had dreamed of this man since that night under the lamps, seven years earlier. It had not happened how she had imagined, but she was on the precipice of marrying him.

If only her father was there to see her marrying the man she truly thought she loved.

But then if he had been, there would have been no Thomas, and they would not have been pushed into this situation…

Perhaps Spencer would have proposed marriage anyway.

But he hadn't before…

Doubts and worries plagued her as she got ready for bed, Spencer having tactfully left the room to give her some privacy.

She wanted to marry him. But did he truly want to marry her? Or would he feel trapped in this union, once all was said and done?

By the time he returned, she was under the blankets, rather nervous about spending the night with him—even if he did seem determined to protect her virtue.

She couldn't quite believe she was at an inn, unmarried, sharing a room with a man. It was all extremely scandalous—and yet there was nowhere else she would rather be. She felt safe here, away from Thomas, away from the life she had thought she would have to lead.

"I will see if they have any extra blankets," Spencer said, wringing his hands. His dark hair almost seemed to shine in the glow from the fireplace. "And make a bed upon the floor. I shan't disturb you—"

Beatrix took a deep breath and tried to be brave, hoping the blush in her cheeks was not as furious as it felt.

"There is no need," she said softly. "The bed is big enough for us both."

Spencer's Adam's apple bobbed as he visibly swallowed. "If you are sure…"

She nodded. "Yes. We will be wed in the morning. It does not matter, surely, if we share a bed now."

As he climbed in beside her she felt the mattress dip, and her heart began to race. He had blown out the candles, but the fire still burned in the grate, keeping the autumn chill at bay, and she could see his brown eyes clearly.

"We shall break our fast in the morning, and then go back to the church. Once the minister has the license, we can be wed, and then you shan't need to worry about Haxbury anymore."

She wasn't sure what made her do it, but she reached out and took his hand. No other part of them was touching, but still he gasped at the surprise contact.

"Thank you, Spencer," she said. "For saving me. I will be forever in your debt."

He shook his head, and drew her hand to his chest. She could feel the beating of his heart, sure and perhaps, somewhat fast. "No. I do not know if I am the right man to be your husband, but I shall endeavor to be worthy of you. You do not owe me anything, Beatrix. I am happy to help you."

He leaned forward and pressed his lips to hers, and the heat within Beatrix grew hotter. He pulled her closer, the blankets caught between them, and his tongue dipped between her lips, making her groan.

Suddenly, she was not afraid. She wanted to be his.

Tomorrow she would be legally, but tonight she wanted to be physically.

His hands moved to her hair, which she had unpinned for sleep, and the feeling of his fingers against her scalp sent sparks flying through her body. She had not known simple touch could feel this heavenly. She kicked the blankets off, feeling too warm to be entrapped by them, and was shocked when their bodies came into contact.

His body didn't feel like hers. Where she was soft and curved, he was all hardness and straight lines. He was still fully dressed, save for his cravat, jacket and boots, but she did not think it would be comfortable to sleep so.

Or to do anything else…

She was shocked to find how wanton a single kiss was making her. Before he got into bed, she had been nervous at the thought of lying with him as man and wife. And now… She didn't even know what she wanted, but she wanted *more*.

CHAPTER THIRTY

SPENCER'S BLOOD BURNED through his veins as he held the soft form of Beatrix in his arms and kissed her in the way he'd been dreaming of since he had first seen her in Vauxhall Gardens, years earlier.

He wanted her in a way he'd never wanted a woman before. Oh, there had been women, he wasn't a monk. But never had he been consumed with desire in this way before. Where he could not think of anything else, could not breathe, could not worry about how broken a man he was or whether he ought to be doing this.

She pressed her body close to his, and while one hand held her head, entwined in those golden locks he had so admired, the other ran down her back, the soft fabric of her chemise the only thing between his hand and her bare skin, and held her tightly.

He was sure she could feel his desire for her, and he did not wish to alarm her, but he could not keep his body away from hers.

His knee slipped between her legs as the kiss deepened, and she groaned. Her hands pulled at his shirt, untucking it, and as her fingers touched his bare skin, they left a fiery trail in their wake.

A loud crash outside the bedchamber door was perhaps the only thing that could have interrupted them. Spencer's nerves overreacted, as they always did, and he jumped away from her, ending up falling onto the hard wooden floor as he did so.

His ardor quite drastically cooled, and panic sending his heart racing, he strode over to the door and pulled it open, needing to see what danger he needed to protect Beatrix from.

But all he found was a scruffy looking lad trying to clear up several broken plates from the floor.

No danger at all.

"What is the meaning of this?" he growled, his ire rising, although not entirely covering his embarrassment. He was not the only half-dressed gentleman stood in the doorway, trying to see what was going on.

"I'm ever so sorry, milord," the boy said, stumbling over his words. "I slipped while collecting the tray and—"

"Just clear it away quietly," Spencer snapped, closing the door and taking a deep breath.

He couldn't bring himself to turn around. What a fool he had made of himself. Right in a passionate moment, he had flung himself from the bed at a loud noise.

"Spencer?" Beatrix called timidly, and he forced himself to turn, and to try to smile.

Her hair was mussed and her lips swollen, and desire roared up inside him once more at the sight of her.

But this wasn't right.

They needed to wait until they were wed. In case she changed her mind and did not wish to be tied to a broken man.

"Just some broken plates," he said, his voice sounding raspier than he had expected. "We ought to get some sleep. We have an early start in the morning."

She blinked, looking both surprised and offended, and had she tried to persuade him into continuing with the direction their night had been heading, he would have been powerless to stop her.

But she did not.

"Very well. Goodnight, Spencer." And then she turned, so he could see only her chemise-clad back in the firelight.

She was probably very upset with him. But she would realize

that it was for the best. Either they would consummate the marriage on their wedding night, as it ought to be done, or she would change her mind, and she would not risk being left with a bastard to raise because of a moment of weakness.

IT TOOK A long time for Beatrix to fall asleep. She felt frustrated. Her body had warmed to his touch, and she'd felt as though she needed something—something which was abruptly interrupted by the loud crash of plates outside the door, and Spencer's decision that they needed sleep.

And that wasn't the only thing keeping her awake. She was also wondering what she had done wrong to make him stop. He had been as passionate in that kiss as she was, she was sure of it— and yet once he'd thought better of it, he'd decided things shouldn't progress.

Was it her lack of experience? Had she done something wrong? Kissed incorrectly? Or had she been too forward, especially when she had pulled up his shirt and touched his bare skin?

Perhaps it had been wrong of her to do so. But she'd felt as though she were on fire, and she'd wanted him so desperately...

She heard his breathing change when he fell into sleep, and felt irritated that he could drift off while she lay awake, very aware of his presence on the other side of the bed, obsessing about what had gone wrong.

And what still could go wrong.

Would he change his mind at the altar, just as he seemed to have done tonight?

Would Thomas discover them, before the vows had been said?

She wished she could send word to Jemima that she was safe, but it was too risky. Thomas might intercept a note, and force

Jemima to reveal where Beatrix had gone, or hurt her in the false belief that she knew where Beatrix was.

Hopefully all would be forgiven the following day, once she was safely wed to Spencer and there was no danger any longer.

SHE MUST HAVE finally drifted off, because she was startled awake by a loud shout. She sat up, immediately assuming that Thomas had come to find her, and was on the other side of the door— only to realize that the noise came from within the chamber. In fact, the cry came from the sleeping man beside her.

The fire had died in the grate and there was only a sliver of light from the moon peeking through a gap in the curtains, but it was enough for Beatrix to see the anguish on Spencer's face. And yet his eyes were still closed.

He threw a hand out, and then a leg, becoming trapped in the blankets. And then he shouted again. A pained cry, followed by discernible words: "No. Don't shoot him. Take me instead."

He had warned her he might have nightmares, but she had not expected to be so moved by them. She hated to see the torment he was clearly in—and had no idea what to do for the best. She could not bear to see him in such pain, and yet she did not know if waking him would be worse.

"Please, no," he pleaded in his sleep, and she couldn't not stop herself from reaching out and putting her hand on his arm.

"Spencer," she murmured, and when he did not respond, she repeated it louder. "Spencer."

His eyes shot open, and for a moment she felt fear in her heart. He did not look like he recognized her. His hand grabbed her arm tightly, and she was about to speak again when he pulled her towards him.

"Spencer, all is well," she whispered, as he clung to her tightly and buried his head in her chest. It was closer than they had been even earlier that evening, when their kisses had almost led to something more.

She could feel how deeply he was breathing as she held him in her arms, but she was sure he was at least half-awake now, since the shouting and thrashing had stopped. Her heart was still racing like a horse out of control, but she held him close, and stroked his hair in a way she hoped was soothing.

To think that he had suffered alone with these nighttime terrors for so long broke her heart—as did thinking of what he must have seen to induce them, and for whom he was pleading. She was fairly sure he was begging for the life of his brother, in exchange for his own.

It was a trade she was glad he did not have the power to make. She did not want to lose him. She had dreamed of him for so long, and now he was here, in her arms, and almost her husband.

She would help him to heal, as she had promised.

"Beatrix?" he said in a muffled voice.

"Yes, Spencer. I'm right here."

He nodded, and let go of the tight grip he had upon her—but he did not roll away.

"You'll stay?" he asked.

She leaned back against the pillows, pulling him with her into a more comfortable position for sleep.

"I'm not going anywhere."

CHAPTER THIRTY-ONE

THE WEDDING WAS a quiet, simple ceremony, conducted with only the minister and two witnesses (an elderly lady who arranged flowers for the church, and an altar boy). It was a far cry from the wedding Beatrix had imagined, in the rare moments over the last few years that she had allowed herself to dream of a wedding. Of course, she had always thought her father would be there. And she had envisioned a new gown, a church filled with guests, flowers in her hair, a joy-filled wedding breakfast to follow.

No, it was not the wedding she had dreamed of—and yet it *was* the groom who had filled her dreams. No matter how they had got here, no matter what they still had to face, she was marrying the man she had always wanted.

And that was why she had a smile on her face as she stood in the gown she had been wearing for two days, with no witnesses that she knew, and promised to love, honor, and obey Spencer for the rest of her life.

They sealed the union with a brief kiss. It was nothing like the fiery one that had consumed them—or almost consumed them— the night before, nor the one that they had shared in her parlor. But it was the first of their married life, and her heart raced, nonetheless.

Finally she was a married woman.

She belonged to Spencer.

She would not have to wed Thomas, and endure a life with him.

Arm-in-arm with her new husband, she walked out of the church, blinking in the bright sunlight which had burnt through the clouds during their wedding ceremony.

She had entered the church as Lady Beatrix Chichester, and exited it as Lady Leighton, a marchioness.

And yet she felt the same as she had done before.

It felt rather anti-climactic to exit the church with no crowd cheering or throwing rice. She looked up at Spencer, wondering if she ought to voice such a feeling, and found him looking down on her, smiling, his cheeks somewhat red.

"Well. It is done," she said.

"It is done. How do you feel, Lady Leighton?"

She laughed. "Like it will take me some time to get use to that name! And how do you feel, Lord Leighton?"

His eyes were open and honest, and he took her hand in his. "Like it will take me some time to get used to there being a Lady Leighton, too. But I am happy. Please do not doubt that."

Her heart soared. Had they not been in the street, in broad daylight, she would have been tempted to stand on her tiptoes and press a kiss to his full lips. Although her night's sleep had been fitful, she did not feel tired. Excitement thrummed through her veins, emanating from the point of contact where he held her hand.

"We should go and collect your belongings, and then we can go home," he said.

Even though she did not wish to face Thomas, her heart glowed at the thought of *home*. It had always been the house that she shared with her father in Mayfair, but Thomas had taken away any warm feelings she had towards the place. Now she pictured Spencer's home, their home, and she was excited to start the next phase of her life. She would go into half-mourning, since she was sure Spencer would not wish to have a new wife still wearing black, and life would hopefully feel bright once more.

"Do you think Thomas will try to make an issue?" she asked, biting her bottom lip.

Spencer hesitated for a moment, his eyes glued to her mouth and slight smile playing on his own lips. "I am not sure. Possibly. But we are legally wed, and…"

He stopped abruptly and anxiety built in her stomach. "And what?"

"I do not like to speak of such things to you, especially in public." He glanced around, making sure no one outside the little church was listening in to the conversation. "But if we were to…*ah*…consummate the union, he could not cause any issues. There would be no argument for an annulment. No judge or minister in the land could tear us apart."

Blood pooled in Beatrix's cheeks at the suggestion, and yet she could not pull her eyes away from his. She swallowed. They were married, after all. And he was just suggesting having the wedding night a little earlier in the day.

And if it made them safer from any repercussions from Thomas…

She nodded, her mouth dry. "If you think that makes sense…"

"Let's return home. We can enter fairly unseen, and decide…what course of action to take."

The coach journey was not long, but Beatrix's stomach churned the whole way. This was it. Her wedding night—or wedding afternoon. The moment when she and Spencer would become one. She just wished she knew exactly what it entailed. And yet she trusted Spencer, completely. With her life. With her heart. With her body…

Just as he had said, they managed to enter the house unseen. Spencer led her through the servants' entrance and up a winding set of stairs that seemed to go on forever—until they suddenly ended with a dark door, that opened to reveal a bedchamber.

Spencer's bedchamber, unless she was much mistaken.

"You have a secret passage to your room?" she asked, because that was easier to talk about that what they were about to do.

Spencer laughed. "It was part of the house when my father purchased it—but I admit I have always liked it. I do like to slip out unnoticed sometimes. I miss the anonymity of being a second son. When you're the marquess, everyone cares where you are, where you are going, and who you are seeing."

Beatrix laughed, but it was hard for her to focus on the words he was saying.

"Would you like a drink?" he asked. "I keep a bottle of port up here—although only one glass, I'm afraid. Perhaps we can share…"

"Thank you," she murmured. Perhaps some wine would calm her down a little.

"You don't need to be nervous," Spencer said, his hand brushing hers as he passed her the glass filled with ruby liquid. "We do not have to do anything, if you do not wish to. I know this marriage has rather come out of nowhere…"

"For us both," Beatrix said with a nervous giggle.

Spencer smiled that heart-stopping smile that she had first fallen for. "Yes. But I did not mean to terrify you, when I mentioned 'consummating', I merely thought…"

"I have no idea what I'm doing," Beatrix blurted out, then covered her mouth in shock. "Forgive me. If you think it is the best plan, I am not opposed. I am simply…uneducated."

He took the glass from her and set it to one side, then took her hands in his. "Then let me educate you."

CHAPTER THIRTY-TWO

H IS DESIRE FOR her took over. They were married. It was done. Giving into his lust for this woman before him, his wife, would not do anyone any harm now. Perhaps he wasn't the right man for her, but he was her husband, in the eyes of God and the law.

Her blond locks were clumsily pinned. He had seen her redoing it that morning in the inn, having removed them for sleep. She did not have the perfect coiffure her maid usually gave her, but she was alluring, nonetheless. The way her teeth worried at her bottom lip, and her cheeks flushed red at his words… It sent a fire racing through his body that was in danger of overwhelming him.

Holding both her petite hands in one of his hands, he reached with the other to release her blond curls, until her whole head of golden hair was free and falling around her shoulders.

"Beautiful," he murmured, and then leaned forward to kiss her. He made sure it was a slow, languid kiss, the kiss of a man who had all the time in the world. A man who was not afraid of being interrupted. A man in love.

She kissed him back with more confidence than he had expected, and pulled one of her hands from his so it could rest on the nape of his neck, sending shivers down his spine.

As his tongue swept against the seam of her lips, he moved them backward, towards the bed, his heart racing and his breeches growing uncomfortably tight.

He wanted to do this right. But God damn it if he didn't want her so badly. He'd told himself he could not have her. That this life was not meant for him. And yet, here they were.

They fell onto the bed without breaking apart, their bodies pressing closer together as the kiss deepened. This time, there would be no crash outside the door—and he had no chivalrous notion that he ought to stop before they lay together. This time, consummating the union was the right thing to do. In fact, it was necessary, in more ways than one.

Somehow he managed to unlace her dress one-handed, without breaking the kiss, and he pulled it down enough to be able to trail kisses down her neck all the way to her breasts, which he kissed through her chemise.

She gasped at the contact, and so he did it again, pulling her dress lower and lower until it slipped off entirely, leaving her in the thin chemise she had worn the previous night.

"I want to see you," he said, breathless. "All of you."

If it was possible, her skin flushed even pinker. "I'm nervous," she admitted.

"You don't need to be," he promised, pressing a kiss to her clavicle before pulling at the hem of her chemise, until it sat around her waist. "You are exquisite." He trailed his fingers up her inner thigh, stopping just before the curls between her legs, and then did the same the other side. She gasped and wriggled her hips, and he could not help but smile.

"Can I take this off?" he whispered huskily, pulling at the thin white garment.

She nodded. "But this feels a little one-sided…"

He glanced down at himself, still fully clothed, his desire for her straining the fabric of his breeches. "Fair enough." He eased her chemise over her head, smiling once more as she tried to cover her rounded breasts with her arms, and then pulled his own shirt over his head.

He loosened the laces of his breeches, but did not remove

them entirely. He didn't want her to feel overwhelmed by the evidence of how much he wanted her.

Spencer took his time appreciating her body, encouraging her arms out of the way and then trailing fiery kisses from her lips, down her neck, over her breasts and all the way to her navel. Her hips bucked and she groaned, and he praised himself for having any self-restraint at all.

And then, when his lips had traveled back to hers, he allowed his fingers to slide up her thigh once more, not stopping as they reached the juncture between her legs. He watched her face color, her eyes close, and when she was struggling to keep still, he allowed himself to breach her opening with one finger, the heel of his palm pressing at the point that was most sensitive.

"Oh, God, Spencer," she groaned, and he thought he might explode then and there like an inexperienced lad. But he wanted to do this right. He wanted her to know what pleasure could lie between them, before he took his own.

Because when he did, it would surely be over very quickly.

BEATRIX HAD NOT known such pleasure existed. Even thinking about what he was doing to her seemed scandalous, and yet the pleasure that was building inside her was undeniable. She needed more. She needed to find out what it was building towards, because she thought she might be consumed by it if she did not.

He pressed his lips to her neck, and she closed her eyes, giving in to the sensations that were overwhelming her, listening to what her body wanted. And it wanted him.

"My Beatrix..." he murmured in her ear as his skillful fingers brought her to a peak she had not known existed.

His words, and the pleasure consuming her, made her heart feel like it might explode.

And then her whole body did. As the white flames of desire

devoured her, she closed her eyes and felt as though she couldn't breathe.

She did not know how long it took for her body to stop shaking, or the ripples of pleasure to stop pulsating through her, but when she opened her eyes, Spencer was lying beside her, a very self-satisfied smile upon his face.

"What—what was that?" Beatrix managed to say breathily.

Spencer chuckled. "Only the beginning."

Their lips crashed together, and he pulled her close once more, and it was only then that she realized he had divested himself of his breeches and there was nothing between their bodies.

Her heart began to race even faster, if it were possible, but any anxiety she had was melted away by his lips upon hers, and the excitement of not knowing what else was to happen.

He covered her body with his, and looked into her eyes as though he was staring into her soul. "You are mine," he whispered, and she nodded. "And I am yours."

There was a little pain, that first time they joined together, but all Beatrix really remembered as they lay together tangled in the sheets was the sheer joy in her heart at knowing that she was his.

Forever.

CHAPTER THIRTY-THREE

ALTHOUGH BEATRIX FELT confident that their marriage could not be undone, she was still nervous as they approached her old Mayfair home.

Thomas might not be able to do anything about it, but that didn't mean he wouldn't be angry or think he could do something about it. She did not want an angry confrontation, and she did not want Spencer getting hurt.

All she wanted was to start her new life, in her new home, with none of this hanging over her.

She was excited about the future—and now she wanted to live it.

"We will fetch your belongings and leave. I promise you, I will not leave your side."

Spencer held her hand and smiled down at her, and her heart felt like it might burst.

Oh, how she loved him. She had not said the words to him, for she was sure he did not feel the same, and she did not wish to say them and not hear them back. It was surely less painful to know in her heart that she loved him and to keep it to herself. And perhaps, in time, he would grow to love her just as she loved him.

"Thank you, Spencer. For everything."

"You do not need to thank me," he said, shaking his head. "Let us fetch your belongings, and then we can go home."

Home. What a wonderful word it was.

Beatrix stood slightly behind Spencer as he rapped confidently on the door. It was, of course, not Thomas who answered it, but their butler Samson, whose eyes widened in surprise at seeing Beatrix. Then the mask of professionalism fell over his face once more, and he bowed.

"Is Lord Haxbury home?" Beatrix asked, feeling as though she really needed to be the one to tell him that she was now married.

"Yes, Lady Beatrix," he said, and Beatrix was surprised to find that she already had an urge to correct him to her new name. She was very happy to be Lady Leighton. Lady Beatrix belonged in the past.

"Good," Beatrix said, more confidently than she felt. "Can you tell him Lord Leighton and I wish to speak with him?"

The butler bowed his head. "Very good, my lady. I will just inform his lordship."

He showed them into the library to wait. It was very strange to be treated as a visitor in one's own home—and yet she *was* a visitor now. Although the butler did not know yet of her change in circumstances, he was obviously aware of the disharmony between Beatrix and Thomas. How much had he raged and sworn and threatened the staff when he could not find her overnight, she wondered.

The sound of Thomas thundering down the stairs sent Beatrix's heart racing. Spencer held her hand tightly, and she was relieved to have him with her through this ordeal.

To her surprise, Thomas blanched at the sight of Spencer beside her, and then turned his angry face towards her.

"What is the meaning of this?" he demanded, his face turning red.

"Beatrix and I came here to inform you that we are now husband and wife. We have come to collect her belongings," Spencer told him calmly.

For a moment, Beatrix thought Thomas might explode. His face turned even redder, and she could practically see the steam coming from his ears.

"Married? What nonsense. You disappear from here for a night, sending everyone into a panic, I might add, and now you return to tell me, your betrothed, that you are another man's wife?"

Beatrix noted that he directed his ire and his questions at her, and not at Spencer.

And yet, Spencer was hellbent on answering every one of them.

"We are married, Haxbury, and there is nothing you can do about it. I appreciate this may be a disappointment, but I'm sure you will get over it. My wife and I will not trouble you for long."

⇛⇚

"MY WIFE." HOW wonderful it felt to say those words. Lord Haxbury looked rather nervous to see him, and Spencer did not think he had to worry about the man challenging him to a duel— again—over Beatrix's hand. For one, it was too late. And for another, the man had not turned up to the last duel. Spencer could see no reason why he would suddenly be brave enough to.

He was relieved that there would be no need for pistols, but he also wanted to leave as quickly as possible. He could tell Beatrix was not comfortable there, and he did not like the way Haxbury spoke to her, with such anger and hatred in his eyes.

As worried as he was about being a good husband to her, he was confident that saving her from this man had been a blessing.

"You make a fool of me," Haxbury said, turning his glare on Spencer. "Both of you. Our engagement has been announced, and now you two are wed—and Beatrix still in mourning, too."

"Love moves in mysterious ways," Spencer said, a small smile playing on his face. "I am happy to meet you outside, Haxbury, if you have an issue with the situation."

Beatrix gasped and squeezed his hand, but Spencer wasn't

worried. Beatrix did not know that Haxbury had not turned up to their duel; Spencer was confident that the man was not brave enough to face him in a fight.

As much as he loathed fighting, and guns, he would defend Beatrix and her honor until his dying breath.

Was this love?

He wanted her. And he would lay down his life for her. But he had thought he was too broken to feel love, to act upon it.

"That will not be necessary," Haxbury said, drawing himself up to his full height. His face was red, but he avoided Spencer's eye. "Take your belongings and leave. But do not forget that I own this house and its goods. If you try to steal from me—"

"I have no intention of stealing from you, Thomas. I simply wish to fetch what is mine and leave you to live your life."

Beatrix scurried away, leaving Spencer alone with Haxbury. He was surprised to find his usual anxieties—well, usual since he had returned from France, anyway—did not plague him. He was Beatrix's husband, and he would stand guard until she was ready to leave.

"Begged you to marry her, did she?" Haxbury said, pouring himself a glass of brandy, in spite of the early hour. He did not have the manners to offer any refreshment to his guest.

Spencer gritted his teeth and ignored the jibe. In spite of being a coward, the man was also a bully and clearly enjoyed pushing others to react.

"Told you how horrible I was, I'm sure."

"I did not need her to tell me. I have witnessed enough for myself, thank you."

Haxbury snorted. "Oh, you think you've won one over on me, I can tell. You'll see, soon enough. Why, only two nights ago the little whore was in my bedchamber, insisting there was no need to wait until we were wed…"

"Enough!" Spencer roared, seeing red. He whirled around to face the shocked earl and grabbed him by the throat. He wasn't much bigger than him, but he was certainly stronger, and

Haxbury gasped. He tried to throw a fist towards Spencer but missed, and Spencer held his neck more tightly still. "You will not speak ill of my wife again. In fact, I do not wish to hear that her name has crossed your lips, in any context. You have your title, your home, your place in society. Make of it what you will. But if you besmirch my wife's name again, you will regret it. And that is a promise."

It was at that moment that Beatrix re-entered the room, carrying a valise and with a larger case being carried by her maid beside her.

Spencer let go of Haxbury, who stumbled away from him, and straightened his waistcoat. "Do you need me to carry anything?"

Beatrix blinked and shook her head.

"Is this your lady's maid?" he asked, nodding to the surprised-looking older woman to the left of her.

"Yes, Jemima. She's been with me since I was a little girl…"

"Well, Jemima. If you wish to join your mistress in her new home, you are more than welcome. I will match your salary, of course."

"So you steal my wife and my servants? Who do you think you are, Leighton?"

"I have stolen nothing. I have offered a choice, and Jemima is free to accept if she wishes."

The wide-eyed maid bobbed a curtsy. "Thank you, milord. I would be honored to accompany Lady Beatrix."

"Excellent. Well, we won't trouble you any further, Haxbury. Good day." He held out his hand for the case the maid was carrying, for it looked far too heavy for her, and his other for the valise in his wife's hands. "Jemima, you may accompany us now, or follow on when you are ready, if you wish."

The maid glanced at Haxbury, and then stuck her chin out a little. "I will collect my belongings and follow you. My thanks, my lord."

BEATRIX WAS SURE she held her breath during the entire encounter. She had not been gone long, packing her things and explaining everything to Jemima as quickly as she could. She had hoped she might prevail on her new husband to employ her beloved maid—but in the end it had not been necessary.

He had offered without her even having to ask.

What had occurred between the two of them that had led to Spencer holding him by the throat? Beatrix had no idea, but she was sure Thomas was at fault.

She might not know Spencer very well yet, although she had shared his bed and now had his name, but she knew he was a good man. And Thomas was not.

Still, her heart fluttered nervously as the door to her childhood home closed behind her forever, and she did not feel calm until they were back in the carriage, the luggage stowed and the horses moving on towards Spencer's home.

Her home.

Everything had changed so quickly, it was hard to know how to feel. She was elated to have escaped Thomas. Hopeful for her future, having heard Spencer mentioning *love* when arguing with Thomas. Sorrowful at everything she was leaving behind—even if she knew she was heading for a far better future. And underneath all of those conflicting emotions, she still missed her papa dreadfully.

"Haxbury won't bother us again," Spencer said confidently as the coach rattled towards their Mayfair townhouse. "I am sorry he was so unpleasant—"

"He has said worse, do not trouble yourself," Beatrix said. "Although when I entered, it seemed he had said something to offend you…"

Spencer shook his head. "I will not repeat it. He will not say it again."

As curious as Beatrix was to know what he had said to make Spencer react so, her new husband clearly did not wish to speak of it, and she did not push him. He had done so much for her; she would trust that if he did not wish to share, it was for good reason.

As the carriage pulled up at the house, she looked up at him and felt her heart soar.

This handsome, strong, kind, supposedly broken man was her husband. And she was ready to start her new life with him.

CHAPTER THIRTY-FOUR

Six Months Later

BEATRIX HAD NOT known that life could hold so much joy. Her household was calm and happy; her husband attentive and kind; and her reputation in society had not been greatly damaged by the broken engagement and hurried wedding. Thomas had rather quickly disgraced the Haxbury name by ruining a young lady with a band of very powerful brothers, and then refusing to turn up to the duel that they demanded—and so he was currently hiding out in the country. Society seemed to think that Beatrix was well rid of him; a sentiment she wholly agreed with. Some even whispered that she and Spencer were a great love match.

Her only regret was that he had never spoken of love again. Not since that morning at Haxbury House, where he had spoken of love moving in mysterious ways. Oh, when they lay together he spoke words of adoration, and he never left the house without a kiss and a promise to see her soon. But he had not declared any feelings of love, and even though she knew she loved him—even more than she had thought possible when her youthful infatuation with him had begun—she did not feel she could say the words first.

Perhaps they would come. His nightmares had improved with her sleeping beside him, by his own admission, and they had not spent a night apart since they had wed. Even when she bled, they spent the nights curled up together, not wishing to be separated.

Although that had not been an issue of late.

She smiled as their boat docked and a footman helped them out. Vauxhall Gardens. They couldn't fail to make her believe in magic. After all, she had married the man whom she had danced with in those very gardens so many years earlier. The man she had dreamed about for so long. The man she had thought would never be hers.

"Would you like some refreshment, before they light the lamps?" Spencer offered.

"Thank you, yes."

On their way to the refreshment table, they were waylaid by two gentlemen who Beatrix now knew very well: James and Timothy, her husband's closest friends, along with James's wife, Louisa. The girl seemed sweet enough, although she was always very timid around them—and around Spencer, especially.

"We did not expect you two to be here," Timothy said. "We thought you enjoyed one another's company above all else!"

Beatrix blushed and could not help but smile at the fact that they had noticed how much time she and her husband spent together. It was surely more than was fashionable, but she did not care.

She loved her husband. If only he felt so strongly.

"It is good to see the world every now and then. And we must hear your news. Is a wedding date finally set, Timothy?" Spencer asked.

Timothy groaned. "You sound like my mother."

"Well, you have been betrothed for what, a year? It is past high time to name a date."

"Not all of us propose matrimony and march down the aisle within forty-eight hours," Timothy said with a roll of his eyes. "Or within a month, like James here." His glance turned to James and Louisa, whose arms were linked. They simply smiled.

Beatrix laughed. "The poor lady will think you have changed your mind."

Timothy sighed. "In truth, I rather think I have. And that she has, too—she has been no hastier about setting a date than I."

"Perhaps it would be better to cry off," James suggested. "Before there is no escape."

"Perhaps. But let us not ruin this lovely evening with talk of such matters. They will be lighting the lamps soon."

Beatrix rubbed her hands in glee. "I do love the lamps."

"I believe there will be fireworks after supper, too," Timothy said, with a cautious glance to Spencer.

Beatrix's eyes also flitted to her husband. His jaw was set, but he did not look like he wished to bolt. Instead he said, "I had heard they were likely."

The lamps were lit to gasps and applause, and no matter how many times Beatrix saw them, she did not cease to be amazed. She took her husband's hand and decided that she would be brave.

"Spencer," she said, turning to him beneath the glow of orbs above. "I must tell you something." She swallowed and took a deep breath. He might not have said it, but he needed to know how she felt.

It was only right.

His brow arched as if to encourage her to continue.

"I do not expect you to feel the same, but I cannot keep this in any longer. Spencer, I am in love with you. I think I may have been since the day I first danced with you, but I have fallen ever deeper in love since we wed. And I thought you ought to know."

His eyes widened in shock, and he took her hand and pressed it to his lips.

"My love," he said, his voice a little husky. "I believed I was too broken to be a husband. Too damaged by the war to feel love. To know what it was. But I know that I love you. You should know it too. I love you. And that I will spend my life making sure you feel as loved as you deserve to be."

HE HAD KNOWN the words to be true for a long time, and yet had not been brave enough to say them. But, when she opened up her heart to him, he had only one answer: that he loved her too. Desperately. And that while he was not sure he would ever deserve her, he would do in everything in his power to make her as happy as she had made him.

Because with her by his side, he felt almost whole again. When they had first wed, he had woken her most nights with his terrors, and she had held him, and he had drifted back off to sleep. And slowly the nights had become easier. She had encouraged him to talk about his brother Jack, and although it hurt, it helped to keep his memory alive. No longer did he dream of his brother's lifeless body, and beg for his own life to be taken in his place.

He would always miss his brother. But he was also grateful that his own life had been spared on the battlefields of France—because if it had not, he would not be there, in Vauxhall Gardens or anywhere, telling his beautiful wife that he loved her.

And he refused to feel guilty for surviving any longer. He did not think Jack would want him to be miserable for the rest of his life.

"Shall we dance, wife?" he asked as the musicians took up their instruments. Beatrix beamed and offered her hand, and they swept onto the dance floor. If others stared because of rumors about their hasty marriage, or because they were so obviously, sickeningly, in love, Spencer did not notice nor care.

Beatrix was his everything.

"I was thinking," Beatrix said as they danced to the thankfully fairly sedate tune. "Perhaps we could think about going to the countryside for a while."

Spencer raised his eyebrows. They had not discussed leaving their London home, and had stayed through the Season without discussing departing. Was she bored of London life? He had not returned to his seat in Wiltshire since Jack's death…and while he thought he might finally be ready to, he was intrigued as to what had prompted this desire.

"I would do anything to make you happy," he said. "But may I ask why?"

She smiled, that warming grin that made his heart feel full, and took his hands as the dance ended. "I feel that it's better to raise children in the countryside."

It took a moment for the words to sink in. The musicians started up again, and they still stood on the dance floor, frozen in the moment.

"Do you mean…"

She nodded and her smile became a beam that transformed her face from beautiful to radiant. "I wanted to be sure, before I told you."

Finally having the sense to lead her from the dance floor, he cut through the dancers with his hand grasped tightly around hers.

"Do you feel well?"

She nodded. "Well enough. A little queasy here and there, but nothing to really complain about."

"Of course we can move to the country," he said, finally remembering to answer her question. "We need not return to London ever, if you do not wish to."

"And you are happy?"

He did not have to think before he answered. He had thought he would never have an heir; that the title would go to some nameless, faceless male in his family tree. He had thought that was what he deserved, having usurped his brother's place after failing to save him in that bloody war.

But he could look at things differently now. Beatrix had changed him—and no doubt this child of theirs, whether a beautiful little girl like her mama, or a boy who would one day take on the title of Marquess of Leighton, would change him further still.

"Happier than I could possibly deserve to be."

Beatrix shook her head, and stood up on tiptoes to press a kiss to his lips, despite the crowd around them.

"You deserve all the happiness in the world, my love. And we will have it—together."

When the fireworks began, he did not jump out of his skin. A shiver went down his spine, and then Beatrix took his hand, and pulled him close, and he watched the colorful lights fill the sky without thinking of the horrors that the loud bangs had always brought to the forefront of his mind.

The war was in the past, and he would endeavor to leave it there. Beatrix, and their babe, were his future—and it was a future he was excited to embrace.

About the Author

Daphne Quinn loves nothing more than curling up with a large cup of tea and a regency romance. She adores the drama and the dresses of the past—even though she is quite happy with all the comforts of the present! She loves living in England and visiting historic sites like the beautiful city of Bath. She shares photos of her visits—as well as upcoming releases and sales!—on her Facebook page facebook.com/authordaphnequinn.

www.ingramcontent.com/pod-product-compliance
Lightning Source LLC
Chambersburg PA
CBHW072128300726
48975CB00003B/973